PAYBACK

JAMES HENEGHAN

Groundwood Books
House of Anansi Press
Toronto   Berkeley

Groundwood Books / House of Anansi Press
110 Spadina Avenue, Suite 801, Toronto, Ontario M5V 2K4

Distributed in the USA by Publishers Group West
1700 Fourth Street, Berkeley, CA 94710

We acknowledge for their financial support of our publishing program
the Canada Council for the Arts, the Government of Canada through the
Book Publishing Industry Development Program (BPIDP)
and the Ontario Arts Council.

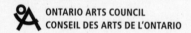

ONTARIO ARTS COUNCIL
CONSEIL DES ARTS DE L'ONTARIO

Library and Archives Canada Cataloguing in Publication
Heneghan, James
Payback / by James Heneghan
ISBN: 978-0-88899-701-2 (bound) –
ISBN: 978-0-88899-704-3 (pbk.) –
I. Title.
PS8565.E581P38 2007   jC813'.54   C2006-905651-X

Cover photography by Tim Fuller
Design by Michael Solomon
Printed and bound in Canada

To Lucy

ACKNOWLEDGMENTS

With thanks to Norma Charles for her input after reading the manuscript.

And my grateful thanks to my editor, Shelley Tanaka, for her patience and hard work.

PART 1

BEFORE

1

My name is Charley Callaghan, but this story is not about me. It's about a boy named Benny Mason.

But it starts off with me.

We came from Dublin, Ireland, about five months ago to live here in North Vancouver. There were four of us — Da, Ma, me and Annie — but now there's only three because Ma died last month, in August. The reason we came here instead of some other place in Canada is because Aunt Maeve and Crazy Uncle Rufus live only a block away. Aunt Maeve is my mother's sister.

Leaving your friends and coming to a new country is a desperate experience, so it is. First there's the problem of starting a new school. Then there's the problem of trying to twig on to the Canadian dollars, the loonies and toonies, the nickels and dimes and quarters, and learning how to use the bus service and the SeaBus and the SkyTrain without everyone thinking you're a totally gormless eejit.

Then there's getting used to biking on the wrong side of the road, and…the list goes on and on.

It's deadly.

At the very beginning of May, soon after we got here, I was wedged into the seventh grade at the elementary school for the final two months of the school year. The woman at the school district office said it would help me settle in with my age group before going on to junior high in September.

Right away I made friends with a boy named Sid Quinlan, but then, in July, Sid and his family moved thousands of miles away, to Ontario. They're gone for good. Probably never see Sid again.

Before he left he said for me to e-mail him, knowing I've got no computer or internet connection but hoping, I suppose, that I'd get one once my da got working steady.

Well, now he's working steady, thank God, but there's still no way we can afford one.

I'm way behind everyone here in technology. Most of the kids have cell phones, too, with instant text-messaging — not that I want all that stuff anyway. I'd rather be out riding my bike.

I'm trying to get rid of my Irish accent so I'll fit in better and be the same as everyone else and make friends easier. The Canadian twang is coming, I think. It's dreadful slow, but I'm working on it. Our Annie is doing way better than me. She's eight, and her Irish accent morphs into almost perfect Canadian whenever she wants it to.

Maybe that's my problem. Maybe I don't really want to lose it. I do and I don't, if you know what I mean.

Ma was terrible sick with the cancer for more than a year at home in Dublin, but that was a long time ago, when I was about the same age Annie is now, and she fought and got over it. She was free of it for the longest time, and everything was grand. Regular check-ups, diet and exercise — we thought she had it beat. Then soon after we came here to Canada it came back and destroyed her.

It all happened so quick. Now she's gone.

I miss her something fierce.

I miss my friends, too. I left them all in Dublin — Sean and Fergus and Seamus and all the rest.

Making friends was easier in Dublin. We all spoke the same language for a start.

And there was a girl, Fiona Devlin. I wrote her a letter, but so far…well, I guess she doesn't miss me the same as I miss her, because it's been ages since I wrote — the same week we got here, as a matter of fact. She sat in the desk behind me in Religious Instruction. Lovely girl, sweet lips, brown eyes. She'd pass me notes that had nothing to do with the subject we were supposed to be studying. I even kept one of them:

Dear Charley, I get more out of staring at the back of yer lovely red head than I get out of a hundred books of common prayer or the catechism. Wouldn't ye think in this day and age we'd be studying something useful like how to behave on a date or how to get a job and look after yer money? Write back what ye think. F.

Maybe people don't answer letters any more, only e-mails or text messages.

It's now sunny September and I'm in another new school, junior high this time, eighth grade.

I don't want to go but my da says I've got no choice. It's not because I don't like school, but not having Ma around makes everything so...well, not worthwhile, somehow.

Annie's the same as me. She used to be full of bright chatter, full of vim and vigor, with enough energy to light up the whole street. But these days she gets home from school and mopes about in front of the telly, not really watching, only half alive, it seems to me. Or she goes straight to her room and stays there until she's called out for dinner.

The other night Aunt Maeve plopped a scoop of ice cream on top of Annie's blueberry pie, and Annie threw down her spoon and burst into tears.

Go figure, as we Canadians say.

••••

Junior high is very different from elementary. It's bigger, for one thing, with different teachers and courses. You move about between classes, so the hallways are always full of kids going somewhere, talking loudly or messaging on their cell phones to only God knows who, and there's gray metal student lockers lining both sides of the hallways. Lots of them have graffiti, cleaned off during the summer but still showing faint ghosts of the original marker-pen ink, so it isn't hard to make out the tags, swear words, pairs of boobs, johnny wobblers and all the other rude stuff.

So I go to school even though my heart isn't in it this year. Also it's still like the middle of summer — bright and hot, with a lovely gold light early in the mornings and the smell of the sea coming up from the inlet. It's grand, right enough.

I've got to admit this is a lovely place. North Vancouver is built on a steep slope facing the sun and the sea and the tall city towers of Vancouver. The mountains are tight up behind us.

And the forest. I love the trees here. Sid Quinlan told me that the snow usually comes to the ski hills in late November or early December, which is one of the reasons he didn't want to leave.

But Sid's gone, as I said, so I'm starting eighth grade with no friends.

Annie spent two months in second grade and is now in third, with a teacher named Mrs. Frederickson, but that's about all I know. Annie doesn't talk about school, and as far as I can see she hasn't made any friends either.

Wednesday of the second week, two kids come up to me in the schoolyard grinning like sharks.

The big one, head the shape of a coconut, goes, "Hey, Red!"

I stare at him.

He yells, "Yeah, you with the hair!"

I know them. They're in my English class.

I remember to try and flatten my tongue the shape of a maple leaf and speak in Canadian.

I go, "You talkin' to me?"

The big one goes, "Yeah, I'm talkin' to you, Red. Who else round here got a head like a three-alarm fire, eh?" He gives a loud, phony laugh.

"The name's Charley," I tell him.

The second kid — long nose, pointed face — steps forward with a sly grin.

He goes, "I'm Rebar?" making it sound like a question.

I don't trust this pair of amadáns. That's Irish for eejits, or idiots. They look like trouble.

I'm not much good at fighting, but I will fight if I'm really forced to it, if my back is up against the wall, so to speak, and there's no other way out of it.

I usually manage to avoid it, though, by bluffing and acting tough.

To be perfectly honest with you, I'm not very brave. Even though I love riding my bike, I'm not much good when it comes to zooming fast down steep hills. I couldn't in a million years ride like my hero Lance Armstrong, whizzing round the bends of the Col du Galibier, because I'd be in mortal fear of crashing and breaking my head.

That's the way I am. Not brave.

Anyway, I'm a bit suspicious and fearful of these two desperate-looking classmates.

"Me and Sammy, eh?" Rebar nods toward his friend. "We really like your accent, Red."

I give them the hard stare. "My name's Charley."

I don't like being called names like Red and Rusty. I like my proper name. These guys are not sincere. They're making fun of me. I already told them my name, twice.

Sammy goes, "Yeah. We figure you're Irish or English or something like that, eh?" He turns to his friend. "Right, Rebar?" Then he turns back to me.

"Or maybe you're from Scotland. Which is it, Red?"

"I'm Irish."

As I already said, these guys are both in my English class. They sit in the row near the wall, opposite side from the windows, last two seats at the back of the room. I sit in the next row, beside Sammy, second seat from the back. The seat behind me is empty.

Rebar is also in my social studies class. His real name is Rod Steel, face sharp and mean like a ferret, tiny, mud-colored eyes close together, razor blade of a nose.

His big friend, Sammy Cisco, has a sneering gob with a lipless slit of a mouth, light brown hair sprouting up from his coconut top, and shoulders like he's got a coat hanger under his shirt.

This morning Mr. Korda, our English teacher, glanced at his seating plan because he doesn't know all our names yet and assigned character parts to be read aloud in the book we're doing, *The Tempest*. We're not doing the whole play, just a special condensed version for eighth graders as an introduction to Shakespeare. It looks to me like

Mr. Korda starts the year using it to check for reading problems.

Anyway, when it came my turn, Mr. Korda, seated atop a student desk at the front of the room, book in hands, elbows on knees, size fifteen brown Hush Puppies up on the seat, gave me the nod and asked me to read.

"Charley Callaghan? You're next." His bushy black eyebrows disappeared under his bushy black fringe.

I knew the other kids might take the mickey when they heard my accent, which could be a bit embarrassing, so I spoke real quiet, making it sound as Canadian as I could.

His eyebrows now in full view again, Mr. Korda said, "Could you jack the volume up a notch, Charley?"

I could feel everyone's eyes on me, so I cleared my throat with a cough and started reading, loud and bold, like I didn't give a monkey's what anyone thought.

It was a long speech by a character named Prospero.

I heard a bunch of kids sniggering.

Finally, I got to the end:

> "We are such stuff
> As dreams are made on; and our little life
> Is rounded with a sleep."

Mr. Korda said, "Thanks, Charley. Well done." Then he looked around the room. "What do you think Prospero, or Shakespeare, is saying about our lives?"

There was silence in the room. After a while, when nobody volunteered an answer, Mr. Korda said, "Anyone?"

Danny Whelan sits on my left, in the middle of his row. Usually a quiet kid who keeps to himself, he cleared his throat. Everyone looked at him.

"Danny?" said Mr. Korda.

Danny blushed. "He's saying life seems like a dream. Like, I try to remember what I did yesterday and it's…gone. Like a dream? Especially school stuff. I don't remember anything we did yesterday in class."

Everyone laughed, including Mr. Korda.

He looked around to see if anyone wanted to chip

in. Some of the others spoke up after that and it got real interesting listening to what they said.

So now in the schoolyard, Sammy and Rebar, having heard me read aloud, are in my face.

Sammy starts. "Hey, Red! That was a great job you did today on — what was it we did, Rebar?"

Rebar grins a ferrety grin. "English dead guy, Shakespeare."

"That's it," says Sammy. "Shakespeare with an Irish accent."

"Well, you've got it wrong," I tell them. "Shakespeare wasn't English. He was born in County Mayo. He was Irish. Everyone knows that. Shakespeare wrote all his plays in an Irish accent."

I wait a few beats but they don't know what to say. I give them the hard stare again, doing my best to look tough, sneering and curling my lip like Humphrey Bogart in a gangster movie.

"Get lost, creeps!" I turn my back on them and slouch away, real slow so they don't think I'm running.

They laugh. Sammy yells after me, "See you later, Irish!"

The next day is Thursday and there's a storm and

it rains frogs, toads and alligators. Everyone's happy to see the rain because it hasn't rained in ages, not since the end of June.

It's too wet to eat outside on the grass in the lunch hour, so I traipse down to the school cafeteria. Sammy and Rebar come over while I'm chewing on one of Aunt Maeve's soggy cheese and tomato sandwiches, which I like.

"Hi, *Red*," says Rebar.

I say nothing, my gob being full of food.

"Red, my man!" Sammy yells, deliberately slapping me hard on the back with one plate-sized hand. I almost choke to death. They stand one on each side of me and toss their lunch bags onto the table, meaning I'm about to have their company for lunch.

"So what brings you to Canada, Red?" asks Rebar. "You running away from all them murders over there or what?"

I don't answer. Instead, I stand and move closer to Rebar till we're practically nose to nose, staring him down. Then I turn and glare at Sammy with my meanest expression, the one I've practiced in the mirror at home.

I can tell from their faces that they don't know

what to make of me for sure. Then I slowly rewrap what's left of my lunch.

"I didn't mean nothin'," says Rebar when he sees I'm about to leave, his tiny eyes mocking.

"Yeah, Rebar didn't mean nothin', Red," says Sammy, grinning at me. "We're only wondering if all the kids in Ireland talk funny like you…"

I can still hear them laughing as I leave the cafeteria.

I don't think I scared them very much.

2

Thursday afternoon and the storm continues.

There's a new kid in my English, Socials and PE classes. He has missed nine or ten days of school. In English, Mr. Korda asks him if he will be comfortable sitting at the back of the room, in the empty seat behind me, and the kid smiles and nods.

He's got a real sweet smile. Also he's got long wavy brown hair worn over his collar, brown eyes and long thick eyelashes like a girl's. He's good-looking like a girl, too, and dresses real neat. No scuffed runners, baggy jeans and T-shirts like most of the boys, but brown suede shoes, fancy green cords, white shirt with a collar, brown wool sweater.

His name is Benny Mason.

The four of us — me, Benny Mason, Sammy and Rebar — form a tight little square in the back left corner of the room.

Right away Sammy and Rebar start calling the new kid names, leaning over and whispering across the aisle at him.

"Hell-o, girly-girl!" murmurs Sammy.

Me and Rebar and the new kid are the only ones who hear it.

Then Rebar starts. "Welcome to our world, fruit fly," he whispers.

"I just love your shoes," says Sammy quietly in a girlish voice.

Rebar wiggles his eyebrows. "How ya like to go out sometime, Queenie?"

"Faggot!" says Sammy.

I say nothing. It's none of my business. Nobody else seems to have heard the slagging.

I would like to see the new kid's face, to see how he's taking it, but I don't want to turn round. I didn't twig that the new kid might be gay.

There was a gay kid named Martin Dolan in my class back home in Dublin, and some of the boys slagged him something fierce. But not for long. They stopped after Dolan bloodied the schnoz of his chief tormentor, a bullyboy named Bramwell, with a Dublin kiss — a fast beano butt, a sucker punch delivered with the forehead. Bramwell didn't even see it coming.

Everyone left Martin Dolan alone after that.

That's often what it takes, a surprise attack against the bullies, and then they usually leave you alone. Usually. They say bullies are cowards but I've never seen that.

But back to Benny Mason. Is he capable of exploding like Martin Dolan and lashing out at Sammy or Rebar — just one of them would be enough — with a good sucker punch or a fast kick to the crotch, hard enough to make them stop?

Who knows? I will just have to wait and see.

To tell the truth, maybe it's a good thing the new kid is gay — if he really is. Maybe Sammy and Rebar will be so busy slagging the new kid that they will leave me alone.

Benny Mason coming into my English class might just turn out to be a brilliant piece of luck.

····

The storm gets worse. The rain comes down so hard that Aunt Maeve drives over and picks me and Annie up after school. Da is away, working the BC ferries in the Georgia Strait.

My da is Tim Callaghan. He's an electrician. When we first arrived in Vancouver, Crazy Uncle Rufus tried to get him a job with BC Hydro. My crazy uncle is a lineman there. My da filled out a job application but nothing came of it. Da eventually got a job with O'Hara's Vending Company in Nanaimo on Vancouver Island, but not as an electrician. Instead he wears a white shirt with a small shamrock logo on the pocket.

He loves it — the job, I mean. His job is restocking the snack machines on the BC ferries. He drives this truck full of Coke and chips and chocolate bars onto the *Spirit of British Columbia*, or one of — what, a dozen? — ferries sailing between Vancouver, the Gulf Islands and Vancouver Island. And then he opens up the giant vending machines and stacks them full of junk food. This means he stays over on the island — in Nanaimo or Victoria — a few nights every week.

Whenever this happens, Aunt Maeve takes care of us at her house. We stay over maybe three or four times a week, sometimes five, depending on what run Da's on that particular week.

Aunt Maeve and Crazy Uncle Rufus have become our second parents. When I was little, before Crazy Uncle Rufus left Dublin for Canada, he used to read me stories standing on his head. He's got red hair same as me and my ma.

Anyway, Crazy Uncle Rufus gets home from work and right away starts acting crazy.

"Stop your nonsense and come inside!" Aunt Maeve yells at him out the kitchen window. Crazy Uncle Rufus is standing in the back yard in his underpants in the lashing rain. "You'll catch pneumonia out there!" Aunt Maeve yells.

Me and Annie, we've seen it all before. We know as well as Aunt Maeve that she's wasting her time, that Crazy Uncle Rufus won't come inside till he's good and ready.

He's enjoying himself in the rain. He stands with the toes of his bare size-twelve feet twisted into the grass, arms raised, head back looking up at the black sky, and long red hair no longer red but the color of rain, plastered to his scalp. And there's only the stormy sky and the pounding rain hissing and gurgling in the downspouts and Crazy Uncle Rufus out there alone with his happiness.

Even though Crazy Uncle Rufus has got red hair like me, we're not related by blood, only by marriage. I love his craziness just the same.

But I can never see myself doing anything like that.

3

The weather is still stormy. Lots of rain and wind.

Benny Mason has been at school almost a week already, but he's doing nothing. He's like me, I guess, doesn't like fighting, except his problem is that he doesn't even say anything. He needs to talk back at them and hold his ground.

In English, Sammy and Rebar whisper taunts across the aisle, trying to outdo each other in nastiness. Benny turns his back on them, pretending he can't hear, but I can see out of the corner of my eye that it upsets him.

The other thing that happened is that me and Benny Mason became partners yesterday in English. I didn't want it to happen but I had no choice. Mr. Korda said for everyone to choose a partner for an assignment on *The Tempest*. The idea was to draw the assignment out of Mr. Korda's job jar.

Kids paired up quickly. The kid I wanted to be with was Danny Whelan, because of his Irish name and because he seems to be pretty smart, but a girl named Birgit Neilsen got to him first.

Me and Benny were the only ones left without partners. Seeing that I sit right in front of him and we were the only ones left, I turned my chair around so we could face each other.

"I'm Charley."

"Benny."

Seeing him close up, looking right into his brown eyes, I really got to see what a good-looking kid he is: perfect features, perfect skin — no zits or pimples — fine brown hair, no gunk in it, white even teeth. He's got the makings of a movie star. Best of all though is his smile. I called it sweet, a word I don't normally use, but it's the only word I can think of that fits.

I suddenly realized I was staring so I said, "I'll go get our project if you like." I got up and grabbed the last folded square of paper out of the job jar.

As I unfolded the paper I said to Benny, "You missed the first week of school. You sick or something?"

He shook his head. "No."

"You new in the neighborhood?"

He didn't answer.

"I'm Irish. Sorry. We never stop with the questions. It's none of my business."

He smiled. "That's okay. I can tell by your accent you're Irish. My mother's dad was Irish. Died about four years ago."

"That's too bad." I thought of Ma. "I've been here almost six months," I said. "I'm trying to speak like a Canadian so I'll fit in better, but it's hard. I keep forgetting. My sister, Annie, she's eight, but she's picking it up real well."

Benny nodded. "Fitting in is…"

I waited. Beside us, Sammy and Rebar were arguing loudly over their assignment.

"…hard," Benny finished.

I nodded. "I know what you mean."

"So what have we got?"

I handed him the paper. "We've got to do a character analysis of Prospero, then present it and lead a class discussion."

Benny smiled.

. . . .

The next morning, as I'm hanging rain gear in my locker, Sammy and Rebar start needling me, asking how I like working with a fairy and stuff like that. They do it quietly so none of the other kids can hear.

I tell them to grow up. Then I notice the word "faggot" painted on Benny's locker.

I shrug. Benny will just have to deal with it. None of my business.

Benny Mason arrives and sees the writing on the door. He says nothing as he opens his locker. Sammy and Rebar immediately start slagging Benny, right there in the hallway, quietly, so no one else hears except a jerk named Tony Marusyk, who just laughs, slams his locker door shut with a loud clatter and takes off for his homeroom.

I watch an expression of misery ruin Benny Mason's face as Sammy and Rebar start in on him, talking in little-girl voices.

Rebar: "Say, that's a cute umbrella you got there, Bennykins."

Sammy: "It's lovely. Such pretty colors."

Rebar: "Pink and blue. They're my favorite, Sammy. I'd just *love* a pink and blue umbrella."

Sammy: "Really, Rebar? I thought your favorite colors were lemon and aqua."

Rebar: "Oh, look, Sammy! Rubber overshoes!"

Sammy: "Very smart, I must say."

They laugh and start prancing about like ballet dancers, waving limp-wristed hands in the air, enjoying themselves.

I wait for Benny to do something, but he just stands there, fumbling about in his locker.

Yell at them, Benny! I'm thinking. *Or walk away! Anything! Don't just stand there! Get mad!*

But he doesn't do any of these things. Instead, he blushes a deep red from eyebrows to neck. Then his eyes start to grow damp.

The tears in Benny's eyes turn my sympathy to disgust.

You don't let the enemy see you cry. Everyone knows that. I feel sorry for him but it's his own fault if he won't stand up to them. Benny has got to learn to take care of himself the same as everyone else.

As I said, it's no business of mine. It's hard enough for a feller to take care of himself without poking his nose into another feller's business.

A bunch of kids come, opening lockers on the other side of the hallway, so Sammy and Rebar rattle their lockers shut and take off, sneering and waving limp wrists at Benny.

These two hyenas scare me, I've got to admit. They're so mindless and mean.

The rain is still lashing down as I get to Annie's school — did I mention that the elementary school is just across from the high school on the other side of the playing fields? Anyway, Aunt Maeve is there to pick us up in her Honda and take us back to her place.

Annie and Aunt Maeve chatter away like a pair of crows, which is a good sign. Annie has been so down. It looks like she's perking up at last.

Anyway, I leave them to it. I don't have to say a thing.

4

The next morning is bright and sunny. The storm passed during the night. When Annie and I get up there's only Aunt Maeve downstairs cooking breakfast. Crazy Uncle Rufus has already gone to work.

Annie is quiet as she plays with her scrambled eggs, pushing the food about on her plate, not eating it.

She's missing Ma. I know it's because of the eggs. Aunt Maeve's scrambled eggs are okay but they're not the same as Ma's. Ma's were lighter and fluffier and had bits of bright green parsley mixed in.

"Yellow and green are the two main colors of the Irish flag," she used to say. "What better way to start the day than with a bit of Irish in your stomachs?"

Have I described Annie yet? In case I haven't she's small for an eight-year-old, maybe even skinny, with serious green eyes just like Ma's, and fine auburn hair

— a color between Ma's red and Da's brown — that falls straight to her shoulders. I've got red hair like my ma but my eyes are neither green nor brown but a kind of in-between color called hazel, and I'm built like a beanpole. The top of Annie's head comes barely above my elbow. Normally, when she's her usual self, she walks lightly, with her shoulders and back straight, nose in the air, like she's a princess whose feet are too royal to touch the common ground. You would never guess we were brother and sister.

Annie is my responsibility. It's my job to get my sister safely to and from school every day, no ifs or buts, Da's orders. Not that I mind. Annie's okay most of the time. She misses Ma as much as I do.

Annie leaves most of her eggs and we set off together for school. Except for a few tree branches and leaves lying about you wouldn't think there'd been a storm at all except everything looks and smells fresh, like the whole neighborhood just tumbled out of the dryer.

Annie drags her feet, like it's Monday instead of Friday, and I briefly consider taking her back to our own house, skipping school together and making it a long weekend for the pair of us.

Then I decide against it. Annie might blab to Da or Aunt Maeve if we skip out. Girls are dreadful blabbers right enough. They can keep nothing to themselves, isn't that the truth?

Benny Mason is absent. The morning drags. I'm in my house-plant mode, my vegetable state.

In social studies I stare out the classroom window, my mind wandering, thinking of riding my bike and my job in the mall and the new cycling shoes I'm saving for.

And thinking of Ma.

Mrs. Pickles — the kids call her Dill Pickles — asks me to stay behind after class.

"I wish to discuss your attendance," she says.

It's the lunch hour. Mrs. Pickles talks as she walks about the room.

"The school year has hardly begun and you have been absent from my class twice already. I've talked with Mr. Bennett, your homeroom teacher. He tells me he's had no notes from your parents explaining these absences, even though he has asked for them and left messages on your voice mail. You were, what, sick on those days?"

"Well…" I start, but she carries on talking.

"That's not all. You have handed in no homework. None. Not one assignment out of..." — she glances at her mark book —"...the three assigned so far on the course. What do you have to say about that?"

"Well..." I start, but again she talks over me.

"And I'm not at all happy with your behavior in class, staring out the window when you should be listening or working. Next Socials period you will sit here..." — she walks over to a desk at the front of the class and slaps one hand loudly on its top — "...where I can keep a closer eye on you."

"Yes, ma'am."

"And after school on Monday you will report to me for a detention class, during which you will begin to catch up on the missing work."

"I can't come after school. I pick up my sister every day. She's only eight, you see. I could come in the lunch hour instead if that's all right."

She asks a bunch more questions and we argue back and forth and in the end she agrees that I come for a lunch hour detention on Monday.

Some of the other teachers have started flagging me as a problem, too.

Payback

So why am I skipping school?

I never used to be like this, honest. It's just that, as I said, I can't get interested in school this year. It's terrible pointless and unimportant to me right now.

I mean, why waste precious time doing things you don't like — school, for instance — so you're supposed to have a better future? How do you know you'll even have a future? We're all going to die — like what happened to Ma, dying so soon when most people live to twice her age.

Is that what Shakespeare means in *The Tempest* when he says we've got a *little* life? Does little mean our lives are short?

Thinking about this kind of stuff could drive a feller barking mad.

It might be different if I had friends. It'd give me something to look forward to instead of all this dreadful business with Sammy and Rebar and Benny Mason. I don't want to be here in school at all.

On the days Da is away from home, it's easy to skip out, because nobody knows what I'm up to, not even Annie. Nobody's home, you see, at our house.

I've always got my key on a cord around my neck, so once I've taken Annie to school I'm free to return to our own house and ride my truly grand Rocky Mountain Hammer bike I bought second-hand through the *Buy & Sell* before Ma started getting sick. Or if it's raining I can sit around at home listening to music, watching telly or reading back copies of the bicycling magazine I borrowed from the school library, or I can take a nap in my own badger's den, Ma's closet upstairs.

I've got the house to myself. No one knows I'm there. The universe goes along without me.

If the school office or my teachers phone home about me and leave voice-mail messages, I erase them before Annie or Da can get a chance to listen.

I'm bad.

....

I don't hang about after school because I always have Annie to pick up, so I don't see too much of what goes on. What I've been hearing lately, though, is that thanks to Sammy, Rebar and their friends, Benny Mason is becoming known through the whole school. Even some of the older kids are starting to call him names.

Payback

I saw this happening a bit on Friday as I was on my way to pick up Annie. Benny was leaving the school, tripping lightly down the concrete steps when a couple of seniors walked by.

One of them yelled, "Hey, Benny! Pacific Ballet wanna know if you're free to do the dying swan for them this weekend."

They all laughed.

5

I do my usual weekend job at the mall — more about that later — and get to school on Monday.

In the lunch hour, I go to Mrs. Pickles' room for my social studies detention and start catching up on my missed homework while I scarf down one of Aunt Maeve's damp sandwiches.

The missed homework is so boring that soon I'm drawing pictures of racing bikes and other stuff with my ballpoint that has three different colors — red, blue and black.

Then, just as a splotch of tomato juice from one of Aunt Maeve's soggy sandwiches parachutes onto my Socials textbook, Mrs. Pickles stalks over and stands over me.

"Do you realize you're damaging school property?"

I look down at the book.

She's right. As well as the tomato splotch, which I'm aware of, there's a whole bunch of doodling all over my textbook, which I'm not so aware of.

I look up at her. "Sorry, ma'am. I wasn't thinking."

"That's your problem, Charley Callaghan. You don't think. You have ruined a perfectly good textbook." She picks up the book and peers at the doodles and the tomato splotch. "You can just take this along to the vice-principal and show him how you waste my time and your own, and how you waste the taxpayers' money!"

"Look, I said I'm sorry. I'll pay for the book, okay?" It's a big expensive-looking book with a hard cover and a million pages. It weighs several tons.

She hands me the heavy textbook and an envelope with a note inside and sends me to the vice-principal's office.

I should've taken the day off. I feel terrible bad about the textbook, though. I meant it when I said I would pay, even if it takes three weekend pay checks.

I'm destroyed for sure. I'm toast, as we Canadians say.

The vice-principal is an old geezer. Mr. Hundle lost his marbles ages ago, everyone says, and he spends most of the day asleep in his office, which probably isn't true but you know how kids talk.

His nickname is Attila the Hundle. That's what most of the kids call him behind his back. He's brutal. But vice-principals in Canadian schools are supposed to be brutal. Like army drill sergeants, they're supposed to scare the crap out of you.

Come to think of it, my old headmaster in Dublin came second to none at scaring the crap out of us whenever the situation required it. His name was Mr. Hayes. His first name was Daniel. We called him — you guessed it — Danny Boy.

He dropped in to each and every classroom about once a month to terrorize us with his mental arithmetic questions. The classroom teacher, also terrorized, kept out of the way by hiding behind the blackboard.

Danny Boy stood up front in his sharp suit and black bow tie and fired numbers at us. We were supposed to add them up. There would be about four or five numbers, double digits, many of them, and when he came to the end of the sequence, he barked out your name and you stood and gave the answer.

If you didn't have the right answer ready it meant going to his office after school and getting a tongue lashing that'd make Superman pee his tights.

I can't figure it out. Adults are free to be happy and do whatever they want; so how come so many of them have got such lousy jobs and such depressing lives? I mean, take a look at most of the adults around you every day. Would you want to grow up to be like them?

Anyway, back to Attila the Hundle. The door to his office is slightly open, so I walk in and sit in the hot seat. He is standing at the window with his back to me, looking out at the schoolyard.

Without turning, he's like, "Go back out and knock."

I'm like, "Sorry, sir, but the door was open. I thought —"

"Go back out and knock."

I get up, march outside and knock on the door.

"Come."

I shuffle back in, put the textbook and envelope

on his desk blotter and stand waiting. He keeps me standing there for ages.

I'm thinking he's got a heart like a plum stone, small and dry and hard.

Then, finally, "It is always polite to knock, boy!" Cold as ice.

I admit he scares me but I'm not about to let him see it.

"Sit."

I sit. He doesn't turn round, just stands looking out the window, arms folded. My legs are jerking, I'm so nervous.

He finally turns from the window, strides over to his desk and sits down. Looks at me coldly through rimless glasses. He's got those deep-set kind of eyes that make you think you're looking at them through a dark tunnel.

"What's this?" Picks up the textbook.

I shrug. It's the same kind of shrug Lance Armstrong gives when he's being interviewed after a day of racing in the Tour de France and the TV reporters ask him what he thinks his chances are of keeping his *maillot jaune* the next day.

Attila the Hundle opens the envelope and reads

the note. Then he looks at the damaged pages in the textbook.

"You admit you mutilated this book?"

I nod, though I think "mutilated" is exaggerating the damage a bit.

"Speak up, boy!"

He waits with tight lips.

"Yes, sir."

It's like we just moved into another ice age it's so cold in here.

He pushes the open book toward me so I can see again my sinful ways. He says, "Tell me why you vandalized an expensive school textbook with these distasteful markings."

I look. I don't see anything distasteful, except maybe the tomato splotch. There's a couple of crudely drawn bicycles in the empty space between chapters, and around the margins of the two pages there's about twenty screaming heads, like the one in the famous painting I like so much — *The Scream*. You know the one — the woman on the bridge screaming, her hands pressed to the sides of her head? Painted by a feller named Eddie Munch? I've got a poster of *The Scream* I brung with me from Dublin.

I got it when Ma was sick the first time, about five years ago. It's on the wall of my room next to my poster of Lance Armstrong.

I've been drawing little screaming heads like the one in the painting ever since Da was laid off from the Dublin gasworks and he and Ma told us we were leaving Dublin and going off to join Aunt Maeve and Crazy Uncle Rufus out in Canada where we would all be better off.

Personally, I think we were better off where we were, in Dublin. Maybe the worry of the move and Da trying to find a job helped to make Ma sick again.

Attila the Hundle is glaring at me, waiting for an answer.

There is no answer so I say nothing.

He's like, "Well?" Dripping cold.

The temperature dips even more. Icicles start to form on the edge of Attila the Hundle's desk. It's deadly in here.

I'm like, "Sir, look, I'm sorry —"

"Sorry is hardly good enough. You destroy a perfectly good textbook and all you can come up with is 'I'm sorry.'"

"I'll pay for the book."

"And tell me why you were having detention with Mrs. Pickles."

"Homework."

"Speak up, boy!"

I suddenly remember what my da told me to do when someone intimidates me or makes me nervous. Imagine them naked. I've got a pretty good imagination so I close my eyes and conjure up a picture of Attila the Hundle sitting there with his skinny white legs and his pot belly hiding his little white johnny wobbler.

But it doesn't work. I'm still scared.

"Well?" says Attila the Hundle.

The room temperature dips even more. The cold is fierce. Frost covers the Socials textbook on the desk in front of Attila the Hundle.

He stares at me, waiting.

I forget what he asked me.

Then he says, "Defacing textbooks and not doing homework are not acceptable behavior at Lonsdale Junior High."

"No, sir."

He glares at me. "And you have two unexplained absences from school."

I say nothing.

"Why?"

"Why what, sir?"

"Why were you absent from school?"

I'm thinking I should maybe tell him that since Ma died I haven't felt like doing much, including coming to school, but that sounds like an excuse, or like I'm fishing for his sympathy, so I say nothing.

Attila the Hundle stands and walks to the window again, hands pushed into the trouser pockets of his dark blue suit. He wears a jacket and a blue shirt with a red tie. He's got thin gray hair and a small gray mustache.

He lets the silence fill the office. Then, after a while, he sits down again behind his desk and opens the folder lying there.

"You're from Ireland, I see. Dublin. Hmmn. Is this the way books are treated in Dublin?" Pause. "You have a sister in third grade at the elementary school." Long pause. "You don't like it here at Lonsdale Junior High?"

"Yes, sir, I like it just fine."

Liar.

I can hear the end-of-lunch bell ringing outside in the hallway.

Attila the Hundle says, "I think perhaps I will have a word with your parents." He stops, leaving a slice of silence for me to help myself to, but I take nothing. He probably expects me to beg for mercy.

I can't even gather enough energy together for a shrug.

Silence. I stare at the name plate on the desk: *Norman P. Hundle. Vice-Principal.*

Norman P. Hundle, Vice-Principal, says, icy-like, "Very well, then. I will contact them right away."

Silence.

"You may go, boy."

I get up and move to the door.

"Boy."

I pause.

"I don't wish to see you in here ever again. Your behavior from now on must be exemplary. If I hear another complaint it will mean automatic suspension."

"Yes, sir."

"And, boy!"

He points to the textbook, pulling a face as though the book is made of dog turds. "You can take this with you."

I return and grab the book off his desk. As I leave I'm thinking a suspension would be just grand — a gift, you might say. I could ride my bike instead of listening to Dill Pickles or my other teachers ranting on about stuff I don't have the slightest interest in. Life would be a lot more interesting if I could get three or four suspensions a week.

But then what would Da say?

I decide not to go back to class. I will give myself a half-day suspension. I grab my jacket from my locker and I'm out of there. A blast of fresh air and bone-warming sunshine is what I need. I gallop down the hill toward the waterfront, my back to the school, my face to the sun.

I sit on a bench at Lonsdale Pier all afternoon, watching the boats and the seagulls. Then I have to run back up the hill because I'm late picking up Annie.

I can see her standing at the top of the steps as I get closer. I wave to her but she doesn't wave back even though I'm pretty sure she sees me, which means she's mad at me. Oh, well.

"You're *so* late, Charley. Where were you?"

"Sorry, Annie. But I'm here now, okay? That's the main thing."

"No, it's not! You don't care about me one bit. You only care about yourself. I've been standing here for *yonks!* I thought —"

"Stop whining, Annie. Come on, let's go."

Girls are such a pain.

6

Lately I've been avoiding the cafeteria at lunchtime because Benny will probably be there and he will expect me to sit with him and I don't want to sit with him because I can't stand it when kids start calling him names. So I go to the woodwork room and eat my lunch there instead.

Then I go to the bogs and Benny is in there, just coming out of a cubicle. His eyes are red like he has been crying.

"Hi, there, Benny," I say as I keep moving, pretending I've noticed nothing.

Whatever problem he's got, I don't want to hear about it.

But instead of saying hi back, he just pushes past me and hurries out the door.

. . . .

Friday, end of the day, I see Sammy and Rebar. They've got Benny over in a quiet corner of the playing field. Sammy pushes Benny into the dirt.

I don't want to see any more, but I'm on my way to pick up Annie.

Sammy yells, "A little dirt will make you look more like a boy."

"Leave me alone," Benny cries desperately.

I watch, hoping Benny will do something, lose his temper, get mad, scream, but he does nothing.

A few of Sammy and Rebar's pals gather, hoping for a fight. But I know Benny won't fight no matter how dirty or muddy he gets.

"Fags are cowards," Sammy jeers.

"I don't believe in fighting," says Benny. "That's why countries have wars. People like you are the ones who start them."

I like the way Benny answers back, but Sammy isn't interested in debating. He gives Benny another shove. Benny slips, this time in the muddier part of the field, and goes down again.

Sammy laughs. The other kids — about four or five of them — yell for Benny to get up and fight.

Benny stands. He looks down at his muddy hands and clothing, and his eyes start to tear up.

"Look! He's crying!" Rebar yells.

The boys jeer.

"Faggot!" Rebar shouts.

Everyone laughs. When they see there's to be no fight they walk away.

I know I should go and help him get up, but I have to run like mad to pick up Annie.

....

On weekends I've got my job in the mall from two o'clock to five-thirty, working in my hotdog suit. I only got the job because I'm so tall and skinny and the suit fits.

I do it because I need the cash. I hate it when I don't have a bit of money in my pocket. Also, I'm saving up for a pair of cycling shoes, the ones with Velcro straps and clips on the sole for the pedals.

I actually don't mind it — the job, I mean — but I don't like the boss very much, a guy named Harvey. He weighs several tons — scarfs down too many of his own hotdogs probably — and he never says anything nice. Instead he complains that I don't play the tape often enough, that I dance like a man who's been dead eleven years — on and on.

The tape is a yucky piece of music that plays out of the head of my suit, even though hotdogs don't have heads. While the music plays, I'm supposed to dance hippity-hop, shuffle-shuffle, hippity-hop. I control the tape inside my suit.

Harvey is right, though. I'm not a very good dancer, especially in a hot hotdog suit.

So that's what I do for three and a half hours, with one fifteen-minute break, Saturday and Sunday afternoons. I dance around outside the hotdog shop in the mall in a sausage suit with "Harvey's Yummy Hot-dogs" on it and every five minutes or so I play the tape and do a funny little dance.

The hotdog suit is made of some rubbery plastic colored to look like a grilled hotdog in a bun with yellow mustard and onions oozing out the sides. I've got a narrow letterbox opening to see through the bun part.

If you don't think it gets hot in a hotdog suit, especially when you've got to dance every five minutes with your arms by your sides with very little room to move them about, then you never tried it. But hey, I like the way people, especially little kids, stop and watch me and laugh at me.

It's the best part of the job.

• • • •

Da is home for three days. He came in Sunday night and picked us up from Aunt Maeve's about eight o'clock.

As much as me and Annie like Aunt Maeve's, it's always grand to be in our own home and in our own beds.

On Monday, Attila the Hundle talks to my da on the phone. Da tells me how much it is for the damaged book. I hand over most of my hard-earned hot-dog money, and then Da writes a check, pushes it into an envelope and addresses to Attila the Hundle.

Da doesn't read me the riot act or hand me a lecture about it, either.

He just puts an arm around my shoulder and says, "If you plan to act mad or stupid, Charley, could you please do it at home instead of at school?"

"Okay, Da, sorry."

"And what's this about missing two days of school?"

I give a guilty shrug.

"What were you doing?"

"Riding my bike."

"And what are these little faces Mr. Hundle mentions?"

At first I don't know what he means and then I twig — the screaming heads.

"Oh, those," I say. "I don't really know. Maybe it's the way I was feeling, you know?"

He knows. He knows how much me and Annie miss Ma.

He's okay, my da. I wish now I hadn't wrecked the book with those little screaming heads and racing bikes and a tomato splotch that soaked through to the next page. My da's got enough to worry about paying the rent and the food and keeping our family going.

"School is important, Charley. Your ma wouldn't want you missing time." He ruffles my hair.

"Yeah, Da, I know that."

I don't tell him in case he worries even more, but my notebooks are full of little screaming heads lately, especially ever since Friday, when Sammy pushed Benny Mason into the mud.

7

The last day of September.

"Charley, what do you think of us using puppets for part of our English presentation? Benny asked.

"Puppets?"

"We'd do it like a TV show, and…"

I didn't listen to any more. Imagine Benny and me with puppets! The other kids would laugh us out of Lonsdale. Especially Sammy and Rebar.

Forget about that.

....

Wednesday, Da takes me and Annie over to Aunt Maeve's after dinner, and then he has to go back to work.

I happen to overhear him in the kitchen telling

Aunt Maeve about the damaged textbook and how I skipped school a couple of times.

"I'm a bit worried," he tells her.

Crazy Uncle Rufus is at a meeting of the North Shore Kite Club, and Aunt Maeve is busy making a batch of her almond and walnut granola. The whole place smells rich with roasting grains and nuts.

She says to my da, "There's no need to get your knickers in a twist about it, Tim. Don't we all know Charley's a dreamer. There's not a scrap of harm in the boy, I swear to God. Stop your worrying about nothing."

It's not the first time I've heard myself called a dreamer. That was what my old Dublin teacher, Mr. Gannon, called me, too. "You're a dreamer, Charley," he used to say when I didn't get my work done on time. Or, "What are ye day-dreamin' about now, Charley Callaghan?" he'd say as I stared out the window at the sky. "What do ye see out there, I wonder? Besides the trees and clouds, I mean? Is it Charley Callaghan ye see? And himself a great leader of the Irish people, uniting our poor country after eight hundred years of foreign occupation, is that it?"

James Heneghan

Mr. Gannon reminded me a bit of my Crazy Uncle Rufus.

I haven't said much about Aunt Maeve. Her full name is Maeve Finch and she's got short light-brown hair that's going gray, and she got a nice easy-going way with her. Aunt Maeve is my ma's older sister, though she doesn't look a bit like Ma. She and Crazy Uncle Rufus don't have any kids of their own. They came to Canada yonks ago, long before us.

••••

There's hardly anyone in the mall at the weekend. I hate it when it's not busy because it's easier for Harvey to spy on me out his window and see if I'm dancing. So I've got to work harder. And there's hardly any kids. No nice-looking girls to admire, either. It's really boring.

Deadly.

••••

Me and Benny are working on our Prospero assignment but now and then we take time out to talk about other stuff. I know a little more about Benny now. For instance, I know he was born here in North Vancouver and that he's got a little five-year-old brother. I ask him what his dad works at.

"Longshoreman. He was killed in an accident at work when I was five."

"That's too bad." Then I remember his little brother. "So your ma married again?"

"I don't have a stepfather if that's what you mean. He took off after my brother was born. So now there's just me and my mom and Rico."

"Rico is your little brother."

"That's right, half-brother."

Sammy and Rebar have been watching us.

"You two sure make a nice couple," says Rebar from across the aisle.

Sammy gives a dirty laugh.

"Screw off," I tell them.

At the end of English as we're leaving the room, Rebar trips Benny, and Sammy pretends it's an accident when he falls on top of him. Mr. Korda helps Benny to his feet and tells everyone to be more careful.

Benny is holding his back. He is in pain. I help pick up his books.

8

On Tuesday, me and Benny are supposed to present our Prospero assignment to the class and lead a class discussion.

I decide to take the day off and get some quality sleep time in Ma's closet instead.

Why do I skip out and miss my part of the presentation?

Well, to tell the truth, I'm scared of standing up in front of the class with Benny.

I can just see it. Sammy and Rebar pulling faces, especially every time me or Benny mention Ariel, a fairy and a servant of Prospero in the play. Some of the kids laughing out loud.

I can't stand the thought of that. So I skip out and leave Benny to do it alone.

Call me a coward if you like.

When I return, Benny tells me that Mr. Korda

gave him the option of doing it alone or waiting to give the presentation when I was there to help him. Benny went ahead on his own. I think he knew why I wasn't there, but he didn't say anything.

Mr. Korda says he will allow me to do a make-up assignment if I bring a sick note, otherwise I will lose the mark.

So I lose the mark.

When me and Annie get to Aunt Maeve's after school she says, "Your da is home for Thanksgiving. He just called and said to go straight over. So I didn't do snacks for you."

We find Da making soup. We can smell it before we even open the door.

He always lifts Annie off her feet in a big bear hug and dances her around the room. He used to do the same with me, yonks ago when I was small, but not now. He knows I don't go for that kind of stuff. I'm not a little kid any more.

It's the Thanksgiving holiday and the weather is perfect. I have a grand time riding the trails on my Hammer. I still do my hotdog job in the mall, and we have Thanksgiving dinner at Aunt Maeve's. Da buys the turkey and Aunt Maeve cooks it. Uncle

Rufus says the grace and I bet you never heard a grace like it in all your life, because it goes on and on and includes most of Ireland's troubled history over the past eight hundred years.

In the end, Aunt Maeve is forced to interrupt him.

"Amen!" she says. "Won't we all die of the hunger while we're waiting for the blessing to be over?"

Everyone laughs.

But it's back to school after Thanksgiving.

At lunch, Benny is about to sit across the table from me in the cafeteria when Sammy and Rebar and Tony Marusyk and another boy named Phil Pitman come over.

Marusyk growls at Benny, "Hey! Nancy Boy!" He keeps his voice down so only his pals and me and Benny can hear.

Pitman and Marusyk don't look at me.

"Hi, Tinkerbell," Pitman says to Benny,

Sammy leans into me and gives my shoulder a friendly punch that really hurts. I don't flinch.

"How ya doin', Red, my friend?"

I tell him, "Get lost, Cisco."

Rebar says, "Hey, Sammy, you believe in fairies?"

"Well, Rebar, I sure do," Sammy says, "especially since our school got its own little Ariel."

Yuk, yuk. They laugh.

Benny Mason stands, humiliated and helpless. Then he looks at me, his brown eyes damp with pleading.

I feel my face flush with shame.

But I've got nothing to be ashamed about. No one else ever says anything. Why should I speak up and stick my neck out?

The guy's got to learn to take care of himself.

He's nothing to me.

9

I said at the beginning that this is about Benny Mason. Not about me and not about my ma, but I've got to tell about her. There's no way out of it. I've just got to get it off my chest.

She was Kathleen Foley before she married Da to become Mrs. Tim Callaghan. Pictures of her taken when she was at Dublin College show how pretty she was. I look at the pictures and it's terrible hard trying to see my ma as a girl — my brain has got to shift some really stiff gears — but it's her, all right, a slim shy slip of a girl with green eyes and red hair. She didn't change all that much — until she got sick.

Da took time off from work last July so he could be with her. He took me and Annie with him every day to the hospital because Ma was dying and soon she would be gone and we would never see her again.

Toward the end Da tried to leave Annie with Aunt Maeve and Crazy Uncle Rufus, thinking it would upset her too much to see Ma's desperate condition, what the disease was doing to her. But Annie started to throw a fit, so Da let her come. The three of us spent every day by her bed, leaving only in shifts to grab a sandwich or a drink in the hospital cafeteria.

Aunt Maeve and Crazy Uncle Rufus popped in for a short visit every day, too. Lots of times, Da went back again and spent the night there with Ma while Aunt Maeve slept over at our place.

Going down in the hospital elevator at the end of each day, leaving Ma behind, I felt like I was running out on her. Da never said much, but he held Annie's hand and hung an arm round my shoulder as we walked to the car. Sometimes, when we stayed late and Annie was wrecked with fatigue, Da carried her in his arms and I held the car door open while he sat her in the front passenger seat and buckled the seat belt around her.

For over a month we watched Ma wasting away. She was like a Polaroid picture in reverse, brilliant color fading away to nothing. She slept most of the time. When she was awake she wasn't saying much, and what she did say didn't always make sense, except for the word "home." She knew she was dying and she wanted to die at home. That was clear enough.

We brung her home and Da and Aunt Maeve took care of her. She didn't last long, but at least she died in her own bed with her family around her.

Me and Annie, we couldn't believe she was gone, that we would never see her again.

We were left only with snapshots. And her things, the closet full of her clothes, where I go when I skip school sometimes and I've got the house to myself to remember the smell of her.

Ma left us.

That was back in August.

Kathleen Foley Callaghan's ashes are now a part of Mosquito Creek Trail, behind where we live, where she'd started to jog two or three times a week when we first got here from Dublin.

After the memorial service, I walked the trail with Da and Annie carrying the urn in my backpack. At a spot by the creek where a small waterfall tumbles over the rocks, Da opened the urn and shook it and we watched the ashes blow away in the wind. Then we sat by the creek and listened to the birds.

I was thinking of Ma, the way she was before the sickness. Now she was a tiny part of a Canadian creek bottom and its soil and a part of its trees and grasses.

Annie was sniffling.

Da said to us, "Your ma isn't gone. She's here." He waved his hands around at the sky and the creek and the trees. "She's here," he said again. Then he put his arms round us. "And she's here in both of you, too. Kathleen Foley Callaghan will never die as long as you both live. Do you believe that?"

I did.

10

It's the third week of October and the weather is getting chilly. But the leaves are great, brilliant.

They remind me of St. Stephen's Green in Dublin and racing my bike with Sean, Fergus and Seamus, the grass buried under piles of leaves. The start of the race was at the park entrance, Fusilier's Arch, only a spit from Grafton Street, and the course went around the pond, past the Garden for the Blind where scented plants are labeled in Braille, past the bandstand and the fountain, past the Yeats Memorial Garden, past a statue of another famous Irish writer I forget the name of, and ending at the big bronze statue of these three spooky women who are supposed to control our destinies.

Here in North Van the trees are different. There's lots of leaf droppers all right but most of them are evergreens — cedars and hemlocks and pines — that drop cones and scented needles on the trails. The smells are brilliant.

I bike the Mosquito Creek Trail all the way up to Skyline Drive, and push through a bright carpet of yellow and gold, my chest pumping with excitement.

My job at the mall is the same as usual. Harvey hasn't fired me, not yet.

School's the same — mostly boring. Sammy and Rebar are the same, too. They leave me alone, but continue to slag Benny. You'd think they'd get tired of it, but no.

I watched them yesterday. Followed by a pack of their new friends, they went up to Benny and started fluttering limp wrists and mincing about in front of him. The pack laughed and howled and Benny ran away.

On Friday morning Mr. Estereicher takes two classes together, an eight and a nine because one of the other PE teachers is off. The floor is crowded while he gets everyone organized.

I see two ninth-grade boys jump Benny, drag him down and pull down his gym shorts. By the time I get there Benny has managed to pull his shorts back up and climb to his feet.

Mr. Estereicher doesn't see anything. He hears the loud laughter, though, and tells the class to cut it out.

....

The next Friday is Halloween.

Da is in Nanaimo, over on Vancouver Island, so we're at Aunt Maeve's place.

Aunt Maeve's house is big, with three bedrooms and two and a half bathrooms. Why did they buy such a big place for only two people? I don't know. Unless it was because they needed the space for all their holy pictures and statues.

They've got Popes, Sacred Hearts and Virgin Marys, St. Anthonys and other saints I don't even know the names of. In the bedrooms they've got Blessed Virgin holy water fonts with built-in night-lights. In the bathrooms there's pictures of St. Sebastian with a whole bunch of arrows sticking out of him, which works pretty good if you happen to be constipated.

There's even a big statue of St. Francis of Assisi in

the hallway. I often touch the bird in his hand for luck when I come down the stairs.

So whenever me and Annie stay over we've got our own rooms. Our own house isn't as big as Aunt Maeve's. Even though we've got three bedrooms, there's only one bathroom. I've got to say, though, the houses here in Maple Leaf Land are enormous compared to the dog boxes in Upper Kimmage Street, Dublin, and they're so comfortable with their central heating.

In Dublin, we rented a "two-up-two-down" house — two rooms upstairs; two rooms down. "Not enough room to swing a cat," Ma used to say. The downstairs rooms were a living room and a "parlor." The parlor became my bedroom. Annie had a room to herself upstairs next to Ma and Da. The tiny kitchen was a part of the living room, and the bathroom was at the top of the stairs. No central heating made taking a bath in your overcoat an ordeal.

Crazy Uncle Rufus wants to take Annie trick-or-treating round the neighborhood, but Annie doesn't want to go. I can understand why, with Ma just gone and everything.

So we help Aunt Maeve give out little Kit Kats and Mars bars. She's got three Halloween pumpkins in her front window. When the doorbell rings we open the door and hand out the treats. Crazy Uncle Rufus is wearing his false eyeballs.

The next morning me and Annie and Aunt Maeve have breakfast together. It's early on Saturday. Crazy Uncle Rufus isn't up yet.

There's a knock at the door just as I start slathering marmalade on my toast.

It's Uncle's friend, Paddy Mullen.

"Is Rufus not up yet?" he says, eyes like a codfish. "We're supposed to be at Gleneagles at eight."

"Rufus said nothing about playing golf this morning," says Aunt Maeve. "I'll go wake him up."

But just then Crazy Uncle Rufus comes rushing down the stairs, talking to himself as usual.

"G'marnin' all," he says. "I'll be right with ye, Paddy." He disappears for a few seconds and reappears with his golf bag. "Let's be goin'." His lips burn skin as they skid a kiss off Aunt Maeve's cheek. Then he rushes out the door behind Paddy.

Suddenly he drops his golf bag and collapses onto

his knees beside one of the garbage bins left outside the door last night because today is garbage pickup day.

Heart attack!

Me and Annie jump to our feet. Aunt Maeve groans.

Crazy Uncle Rufus, elbows on the dustbin, bows his head and joins his hands together.

"I forgot me friggin' prayers!" he yells.

It's not a heart attack.

Crazy Uncle Rufus makes a lightning-fast sign of the cross and then, elbows still on the garbage bin, jabbers his prayers in a long muddled stream of words, eyes closed tight, hands joined together in front of his nose.

"I'll be in the car," says Paddy, rolling his eyes.

Aunt Maeve looks at me and Annie and shrugs her shoulders.

"Didn't I marry an amadán?" she says with a smile.

Crazy Uncle Rufus' prayers gallop to a finish. He crosses himself quickly and then jumps into Paddy's SUV.

We watch it till it's out of sight.

We go back to our breakfast — Aunt Maeve to her boiled egg and me to my toast and marmalade.

Before she starts back on her corn flakes, Annie smiles over at me.

I can see Ma smiling at me out of Annie.

• • • •

I've got the damaged Socials textbook in my room at Aunt Maeve's. It's mine now. I paid for it. I can throw it out with the rubbish if I want.

But I don't. I lie on my bed, leafing through its pages until I find my doodles, the bikes and the screaming heads.

Then I look at the section dealing with World War II, at the pictures of planes and tanks and famous people. I like to read about WWII. It's really interesting.

When I was Annie's age I used to make airplane models from kits. I made a Spitfire and a Hawker Hurricane and a Messerschmitt and hung them from my ceiling. I liked to look at them swinging above my head and imagine myself behind the controls of the Mark V Spitfire in a dog-fight high above the

English Channel, soaring and diving, firing my two 20-millimeter cannons and four .303 machine guns at the German Messerschmitt.

I didn't bring my models with me to Canada. Ma wouldn't let me. No room, she said. Every inch of space is precious. Besides, they'll get broken.

I argued but it didn't do any good.

I was pissed off with her then.

In the textbook there are pictures of Hitler, the evil leader in Germany, and Winston Churchill, the heroic English leader. There's pictures of death camps and prisons, where Hitler had millions of Jews slaughtered in gas ovens. There's a picture of a starving skeleton of a man looking through barbed wire in Buchenwald, one of the death camps.

Underneath the man's picture it says:

In Germany they first came for the communists, and I didn't speak up because I wasn't a communist. Then they came for the Jews, and I didn't speak up because I wasn't a Jew. Then they came for the trade unionists, but I didn't speak up because I wasn't a trade unionist. Then they came for the Catholics, and I didn't speak up because I wasn't a Catholic. Then they came for me — and by that time there was nobody left to speak up.

— Martin Niemöller (1945).

Spent seven years in a concentration camp.

11

On Monday there's a fire drill.

The alarm goes off during first class. We move our butts. The school empties in less than two minutes.

Attila the Hundle stands at the door timing the evacuation with his silver pocket watch like it's an Olympic event.

We jostle and fidget in the school yard, about eight hundred of us, and watch the North Vancouver Fire Department rush into the school.

When the bell rings the all-clear, everyone traipses back into the school.

The next day, Tuesday, the fire alarm goes off again.

We do a repeat of the day before, hanging around like a swarm of homeless bees, the weather colder, lots of kids with earphones as they listen to their music.

Unbelievably, the alarm goes off again on Wednesday. For the third time the school empties out into the cold schoolyard.

I'm thinking there's no way that three consecutive alarms can all be fire drills, but maybe it's the Canadian way, a fire-alarm fever. It's becoming a regular event.

Our long hot summer and fall came suddenly to an end shortly before Halloween and now it's wet November and we stand shivering outside in the cold drizzle as we watch the firemen come and go. The teachers twitch and stamp impatiently as they check their class lists, making sure nobody's left in the building even though they know it's most likely a false alarm.

The alarm rings again the next day, Thursday. The teachers are ticked off, I can see it in their faces.

We all jostle and push our way along the halls, out to the cold school yard. We're not allowed to go to our lockers after an alarm sounds, but lots of kids are starting to ignore that rule, snatching sweaters and jackets before plunging outside into the cold.

I don't bother. Wasn't I brung up in Dublin, the coldest, wettest place in the universe?

We're all expecting another interruption on Friday, but the morning goes by and nothing happens.

During the first afternoon period, science, I decide to take a trip to the bogs — washroom in Canadian, which is a joke of a name because hardly anyone goes there to take a wash.

I turn the corner in the deserted hallway…

Jeez!

It's himself — Benny — standing next to the fire alarm, looking around to see if anyone's watching.

He sees me and freezes.

I stay where I am, not moving. He looks at me and slowly, deliberately reaches out and pulls the alarm. Then he turns and hurries away while the ear-splitting bells clang for the fifth consecutive day in the hallways of Lonsdale Junior High.

Who would ever have thought of Benny Mason?

I'm gobsmacked!

So Benny is the one with the fire-alarm fever. Benny is the perp, as they say here.

Who would ever guess? You wouldn't think he had it in him to cause such ferocious commotions.

I'm not only gobsmacked, I'm totally blown away!

So now what do I do? Tell Attila the Hundle? Tell him I saw Benny pull the fire alarm?

No. I don't want to get Benny in more trouble. There's an unwritten code in school that you don't fink, snitch, tattle, tell tales on other kids.

It's always been that way. I guess you could call it a code of honor. Everyone, far as I know, believes this to be true.

But I can't forget the cold, unseeing look in his eyes just before he pulled the alarm.

I don't know what to do. Maybe I shouldn't tell anyone.

For now, anyway.

••••

Saturday afternoon and I'm dancing about in my hotdog suit as usual. But it's not my usual slick, crowd-pleasing performance and I keep forgetting to play the tape, and that drives Harvey crazy.

I think he'll fire me pretty soon.

On Sunday, Harvey keeps charging out of the shop.

"Put a sock in it, Irish! If you don't want to do the job I can find someone else who will, ya hear me?"

Later, I ask Aunt Maeve what she thinks about someone at school pulling the fire alarms every day for a whole week.

"Someone actually did that, Charley, every day?"

"That's right."

"Do they know who it is?"

"Not yet."

"Well, I hope they catch whoever it is and help him. Or her."

"Help him?"

Aunt Maeve nods. "Someone does that, seems to me it's a cry for help."

12

It's the day before Remembrance Day, which is when all the schools have their "Lest We Forget" ceremonies because tomorrow's a holiday.

Assembly, eleven o'clock in the gym.

The kids stand. Teaching staff sit in chairs up on the stage, red poppies in lapels.

The school band plays John Lennon's "Imagine." Then Principal Wood says a few words, followed by Mr. Korda. He's a good speaker. He tells us about how many people died in the First World War. He is not reading from a script or from notes.

"They said it was a war to end all wars," said Mr. Korda. "But then only twenty-one years later came World War Two. Adolf Hitler and his Nazis in Germany were taking over the whole of Europe, bombing, destroying, killing, sending millions to the death camps. They had to be stopped. Canada and the United States joined with England to fight this terrible evil. Many more people died to preserve our precious freedom. That's why we're here today. To remember. To remember the sacrifice of those soldiers, sailors, airmen and women who gave their lives."

Mr. Korda walks to the back of the stage and sits down.

Silence.

The band plays again.

I'm still worrying about whether I should snitch on Benny pulling the fire alarms. Maybe I should and that would be the lead-in to telling about all the other stuff.

"A cry for help," Aunt Maeve said.

So what's stopping me?

••••

Monday afternoon. Socials first period. We're all sitting quiet as mushrooms in the semi-darkness. I'm supposed to be taking notes from the overhead projector but I'm drawing little screamers in my notebook as usual, when an office messenger knocks on the door.

Dill Pickles opens the door and then announces for all to hear, "Benny Mason, the vice-principal would like to see you in his office right away."

They've got him. They've got the fire-alarm psycho. They've got Benny.

So now I can stop worrying. The problem is in someone else's hands.

It makes sense. All they needed last week was for every teacher to keep a list of classroom absences, visits to the bogs, usually. Who was out of what classes during the times the alarms went off. It was only a matter of time before Benny was caught, stands to reason.

As I look across the room at Rebar I'm imagining Benny in the vice-principal's office at this very moment, in the hot seat, with Attila the Hundle questioning him about the fire alarms.

I'm so busy imagining the scene in Attila the Hundle's office that I pay very little attention to the words rolling up on the screen or the notes I'm supposed to be copying into my book as Dill Pickles writes a whole bunch of desperate stuff about the British North America Act of 1867 on the overhead projector. I eyeball the door every two seconds, waiting for Benny to return, anxious to see his face.

But at the end of the afternoon the final bell rings and Benny still isn't back from the vice-principal's office, and by now I've got hundreds of little screaming heads crowded together on one page.

Eddy Munch must be turning in his grave, knowing I've turned his one-woman horror show into a global scream.

I head out into the schoolyard and wait for Benny, near the office where I will see him coming out. But I can't wait long because of Annie.

Just when I'm thinking that I can't wait any longer, Benny comes out, his face pale and wooden. Rigid, like he had a brutal time with Attila the Hundle.

"You okay?" I ask him.

He stands staring at me, the muscles working his jaw.

"Benny? You okay?"

He stands staring at me, not wimpy and crying the way he usually is. The difference is in his eyes and the tight muscles working his jaw.

He looks at me like he doesn't really see me.

"Benny?" I say. His name feels awkward in my mouth. I've never called him by his name before. "You okay?"

He stares at me, but I'm sure he's not seeing me. Then he turns suddenly and walks off, leaving me standing there.

He keeps on going, not looking back.

I watch his back, straight as a soldier's, as he walks away.

••••

Benny is not at school on Wednesday.

On Thursday a body is washed up onto the beach at English Bay.

It's the body of a teenager.

It's Benny.

••••

A terrible tragedy. That's what they're calling it on the telly's evening news:

"The boy who leaped off the Lions Gate Bridge into the cold gray waters of Burrard Inlet yesterday afternoon has now been identified as Benjamin Mason, thirteen years old," says the newsreader. "The boy was seen Wednesday by several commuters in their cars. By the time the police got to the spot it was too late…"

Benny is dead.

13

Lonsdale Junior High is quiet as a church. The hallways are almost silent, kids whispering together as they open and close locker doors like they're made of glass.

After lunch Mrs. Wood calls for an assembly in the gym, which makes it two assemblies in the same week.

The teachers sit on chairs in a line at the back of the stage. They look sad. Attila the Hundle isn't there.

There's a lectern and a microphone set up on the central edge of the stage. Mrs. Wood says a few solemn words about what a terrible tragedy it is to lose Benny Mason.

Then she tells us that Benny Mason was a troubled boy. Benny took his own life. But Lonsdale Junior High failed Benny. We're all responsible, she tells us.

Benny left a note in his room at home. His ma found it. Mrs. Wood doesn't tell us what was in the note Benny's ma found except that her son was bullied at school. School counselors will be following up with classroom sessions on bullying in the coming weeks.

I glance across at Sammy. His usual sneer looks uncertain.

I used to be afraid of Sammy and Rebar. But right now I hate them.

Most of all I hate myself.

We all killed Benny.

I'm destroyed with the thought of it.

Someone drops a cell phone onto the gym floor and the effect is like a bomb going off.

I don't wait to listen to what anyone has to say. I've got to get away, out of the gym and into the clean air.

I push my way out through the crowd. Instead of returning to class I snatch my jacket out of my locker. I'm out of there.

I head down the hill to Lonsdale Market and sit outside on the pier. It's windy and gray and cold. I watch the SeaBuses churning back and forth through the choppy waters to and from Vancouver's office towers, and then I watch a pair of seagulls fighting over a scrap of food.

Shame and guilt push up inside me, growing and filling the empty spaces around my lungs and heart. There's ferocious black clouds around my head and shoulders, pressing me down.

I sit there for a long time.

Shivering with the cold, I get up and start back up the hill toward the elementary school. I can't be late picking up Annie.

I make it to Lonsdale Elementary soon after three o'clock. Annie and two other girls are drifting down the steps in a tight, chattering bundle.

I'm happy to see she is making some friends.

"Let's go, Annie," I yell.

Her new friends shout goodbyes — all squeaky and twittering, the way girls always do, you know — as she runs to me and pulls me away and we start for home.

Knots of high school kids are already making their way across the high school playing fields toward the road. Lots of them pass the elementary school on their way home. I hear the name Benny Mason mentioned more than once.

"That's awful about Benny Mason," says Annie.

"It is, Annie, right enough."

"I liked him. He was nice."

"You knew him?"

"Yes. I dropped my book bag on the steps one time and it rolled down and a really mean boy named Gilbert Graves who I hate gave it a kick and spilled almost everything out. Anyway, Benny Mason was coming across the sports field and saw me and he helped me pick up my stuff and he told me his name and everything and then he asked my name and I told him and he asked if I have a brother at the junior high and I said yes and he said he knows you."

Annie manages this in one breath. She drops into her Dublin patter more when she talking to me or Da. It's like she speaks two different languages.

"How could he do a thing like that, Charley?" she says. "I don't understand."

She's still talking about Benny Mason.

"I don't twig either, Annie."

Aunt Maeve's got a snack waiting for us as usual — raw veggies, cheese, Melba toast.

Annie says, "I'm sick of raw broccoli and

cauliflower, Aunt Maeve." She turns to me, groaning. "Wouldn't you love a Chocolate Kimberley right this very minute, Charley? Or a slice of Fogarty's pepperoni pizza?"

"Well, there are no Chocolate Kimberleys in Vancouver," Aunt Maeve says. "And this is Finch's, not Fogarty's, so you'd better deal with it. Broccoli's better for you. anyway. You're a growing girl. You need veggies and fruit at your age, not cookies and pizza."

Aunt Maeve is extra strict since Ma died, and she takes looking after us pretty seriously.

I hurry up the stairs to my room — not the one with the Lance Armstrong poster and *The Scream* but the one in Aunt Maeve's with the picture of the Sacred Heart and the Blessed Virgin holy water font and nightlight.

I don't want to talk to Aunt Maeve. Don't want to talk to anyone, period.

I throw myself on the bed and stare at the ceiling and think about Benny leaping to his death off a bridge deck far above the swirling gray sea.

I remember how he looked at me just before he pulled the fire alarm.

Payback

I could have saved him. I could have gone to the counselor or the principal. I could have stuck up for him against Sammy and Rebar and the others.

I'm destroyed.

It's like I pushed him off the bridge.

PART 2

AFTER

1

It's the second week of November and the snow on the mountains is early, everyone says.

Saturday morning I pedal my Hammer up the switchback road to the snowline on Mount Seymour.

I pretend I'm Lance Armstrong. I've broken away from the peleton and my team-mates and I'm dancing on the pedals as I zoom up the Col du Galibier.

I don't make it to the parking lot at the top of Seymour because of the snow. So I stop, pull on an old hoodie and ride back down, braking before the curves, taking it slow and easy in case there's black ice on the road.

My weekend hotdog routine has become deadly dull. I know it, even though I do my best to pretend it's show-time and I'm the hottest hotdog in town.

Sunday, a little girl stands watching me. She's about six. Her mother wants to move on but the little girl refuses to budge, pulling on her ma's arm. I turn on the music.

After I finish my dance the little girl says, "That was stupid. I hate you!"

Her mother finally pulls her away, and I watch them walking off down the mall.

Harvey pops his head out and yells, "I'm watching you, Callaghan. I'm watching you!"

••••

When me and Annie get home from school we're happy to see Da's Chevy in the driveway. When Ma was there for us it didn't matter so much that Da was away. But now things are different. Aunt Maeve is our second ma and Crazy Uncle Rufus is our second da, but it just isn't the same as having your own folks waiting for you when you get home.

Da's whistling as he bakes a casserole for dinner. Da likes to cook. He stops for the few seconds it takes for Annie's usual bear hug and dance, and then he goes back to it, talking as he works.

"How's things, kids? How's school? You glad to see your old man?"

Annie becomes a chatterbox. "A boy from Charley's school killed himself."

"No! Really?" He looks at me. "Who was he, Charley?"

"Benny Mason. Eighth grader."

"You knew him, Charley?"

Shrug. "He was in a couple of my classes."

"What happened? How did he kill himself?"

"He jumped off the Lions Gate Bridge," Annie says.

Da stops working at the kitchen counter and turns to face us, mouth open in astonishment.

"The Lions Gate Bridge! Jeez! Pardon me. Why'd he do a thing like that?" He stares at me in astonishment. "What was his problem, Charley?"

My throat seizes up something fierce. I cough to clear it and then I say, "Bullying. He killed himself because he couldn't take all the bullying. That's what they're all saying."

Da frowns. "God rest his soul, the poor lad."

He turns back to his work at the counter, still asking questions about Benny Mason, but I slide away and escape upstairs to my room and lie on my bed and look at my picture of Ma on the chest.

It was taken soon after I was born. She's holding me in her arms. Ma looks young.

I look at the picture a lot. When I look in the mirror I can see that I look a lot like her. Same red hair, same mouth, except in this picture she's got a faraway look in her green eyes, like she sees something no one else can see.

Maybe that's the way I look, too, when I'm...

"Daydreaming again, Charley?"

"Hi, Ma."

"Your da is proud of you, Charley. And he loves you. You mustn't be afraid to talk to him when things bother you."

Did I mention that Ma drops in now and then to offer a word or two and cheer me up?

Well, she does. I didn't like to mention it earlier for fear I'd be thought barking mad, but she's here again now, standing in the doorway wearing her gray track suit. Her hair is untidy, the red curls blown by the wind, like she just got back from her jog.

"I want us all to be back home together in

Dublin, Ma. With things the way they used to be. I don't like it here without you."

"I'm still here, Charley. I haven't left you. I will always be with you. As for Vancouver, it's a grand place. Don't you just love the mountains and the trees? And the air? You've got to give it a chance, Charley."

"I miss Dublin. I miss my old pals and the old neighborhood. I miss walking up the Liffey Quays and Temple Bar and Grafton Street and across the O'Connell Street Bridge and lying in the grass in St. Stephen's Green and —"

"I know you do, Charley. But sometimes we have to leave things behind. You will get to love it here, I promise."

"I never heard back from Fiona. You remember Fiona? I wrote —"

"Ach, don't worry your head over the little madam. There'll soon be plenty of nice girls for you. Another couple of years and they'll all be falling over themselves for you to notice them."

I look at my posters on the wall of *The Scream* and of Lance Armstrong racing his bike in the Tour de France.

Lance is from Texas. Texans are tough. Lance was once very sick with the same kind of disease Ma had. It could've killed him but he beat it and came back from it to win the Tour de France seven times in a row, something no one has ever done before.

The Tour is the toughest sporting event in the world. After Ma, Lance is my number one hero, the toughest Texan of all, not just because he won the Tour de France so many times, but because he fought the disease every inch of the way so he could be a champion, never giving up, and training on his bike when he could hardly walk ten steps.

I wish I could be like Lance Armstrong instead of the way I am. Lance is the kind of feller who would speak up if he saw discrimination or injustice.

"Ma —"

But she's gone.

When Annie comes into my room to tell me dinner will be ready in a few minutes, she asks me why I'm crying.

"I'm not crying," I tell her.

But I am. Annie lies down beside me and presses her head to my shoulder and puts her skinny arms around me.

2

The memorial service for Benny Mason takes place early in the morning outside a small chapel near the waterfront a week after his death.

The day is bright. A low fog hangs over the inlet. The tops of the distant city towers on the opposite shore rise out of the fog, and they look like the way they paint heaven in holy pictures.

There's a big turnout of kids from the school but I don't see Sammy or Rebar. The air smells sharp and cold. Frost glistens on the grass.

The TV fellers are here with their cameras. The story of Benny's death has been in all the papers and on the telly.

Annie is in school, but Aunt Maeve is here and a bunch of people from the neighborhood. There's an important-looking short fat man in a black overcoat who I later find out is on the city council. Attila the

Hundle isn't here but Mrs. Wood is, and also Mr. Estereicher.

It's not hard to spot Benny's ma. Mrs. Mason is wearing a long dark coat, a black hat with a veil that hides her face, and black gloves. She stands with her feet together, black shoes, at attention almost.

Clutching the folds of her coat with one hand is a little boy. Benny's brother, I guess — dark hair, big dark eyes, dressed neatly in a windbreaker. He doesn't look like Benny.

Then I notice Ma. She's standing back from Mrs. Mason. She's wearing her "good" brown wool skirt and the black leather jacket, the one she bought in Dublin which she hardly ever wore.

She sees me look across at her, and she smiles and waves at me.

I'm sorry I've come to the service. It feels like they all know the truth about me. Their eyes say it all. *Look, there's Charley Callaghan. It turns out that he knew all along about the bullying and he never said anything.*

I do my best to shrink my skinny frame behind Aunt Maeve's plump figure whenever a camera swings in my direction.

Payback

At least there's no coffin, thank God, and there's no hole dug in the earth. I went to a funeral once, in Dublin. It was a relative of Da's, a distant cousin, and everyone lined up to look at the dead man lying in his coffin.

I didn't line up. There was no way I wanted to see a dead guy.

So I was especially afraid of being forced to look inside a coffin at Benny's drowned face. I couldn't have stood that.

I've been having nightmares about it.

The minister is speaking. He is a big man with a big stomach, pregnant with holy piety my da always says if he sees a priest or minister with a big belly.

I look for Ma but she's gone.

The minister is saying a bunch of nice things about Benny, like what a good son he was and what a good brother and all that kind of stuff, but how would he know? Nobody knew Benny — not the minister, not Benny's mother, not me. Nobody knew him. If they did, then why didn't they stop him from jumping?

He reads some passages from his book.

My eyes keep coming back to Benny's ma. Mrs. Mason stands very still.

Is she staring at me from behind that veil? Does she know?

The reading seems to go on forever. I can't wait for the service to be over.

I feel Ma's hand on my arm. She looks nice in her black jacket.

"Hi, Ma. Did I tell you?"

"Tell me what, Charley?"

"About Benny. The name-calling, the bullying. I didn't speak up. Aren't you terrible ashamed of me?"

"I'm never ashamed of you, Charley."

The minister finishes reading and that's it. The end of the service. No other people come forward to speak.

I turn again to speak to Ma, but she's gone.

····

The nightmares crucify me. Benny's drowned face with its staring eyes. As I struggle to get away, Benny reaches out to grab me and that's when I wake in a sweat, gasping for breath, bed covers tangled about my legs.

Payback

Last night when Benny reached out to grab me he had no eyes, only baby crabs crawling out of the empty sockets.

Deadly.

3

Today I'm skipping school. Da's away and I have the house all to myself.

Did I mention how I sometimes lie down in Ma's closet with the light out and the door partly closed? And breathe the smell of her? And did I mention that her jackets and coats have got strands of her hair on the lapels and collars?

Anyway, that's what I do this afternoon after riding the trails on the lower slopes of Cypress Mountain for a couple of hours. I fall asleep in the closet and when I wake up it's almost three o'clock and I've got to rush over to the school to pick up Annie, and then take her with me to Aunt Maeve's.

Ever since the memorial service I keep seeing Mrs. Mason, standing at attention in the grounds of the chapel, with Benny's kid brother clutching her dress. I can't get them out of my mind.

I found out where she lives. So later, while Annie is scarfing down her after-school snack, I dodge out the back and jump on my bike and less than five minutes later I'm standing on the street across from Benny Mason's house.

I stay for several minutes, sitting astride my bike, noticing the details of the house. Weathered gray cedar siding, gray cedar fence interrupted by a collapsed gate, gray sagging porch, untidy rat's nest of a front yard wild with dead thistles and long grass, empty driveway.

Everything about the place looks gray and run-down except for three windows with bright red curtains.

The house has no basement. I don't see anything of the ma or the little boy. The place looks empty except for the curtains.

I head back to Aunt Maeve's place.

Nobody missed me.

Crazy Uncle Rufus says grace, never quite the same. "For what we are about to receive, Lord —

Maeve's wild coho salmon and green salad, even though she knows I detest salad and don't have a very high opinion of fish either, wild or tame, but she's a good woman, as You know, and she does the best she can with this poor excuse of a husband and these two lovely children, preparing nutritious repasts for us, the likes of which would tempt the palates of Ireland's ancient kings and poets — may we all be truly thankful. Amen."

"Amen," we answer, even though me and Annie don't understand half of what he says.

As soon as dinner is over I say I'm going to my room to do homework. By now it's pretty dark outside but I sneak out and jump on my bike again and zoom back to the Mason house. Driveway still empty, so probably no car, unless it's one of the ones parked in the street, which seems unlikely when you have a whole driveway. Light shines from behind the curtains.

I stand for a while, leaning on my bike, watching.

A man steps out of the night, giving me a ferocious fright. He's wearing a dark track suit. Gives me a hard look and I fall back, scared out of my socks and almost falling over my bike.

The man moves on. He is big with a thick black beard, the kind of feller you see on the telly, on the Friday night wrestling show, or in a horror flick.

That big sucker made my heart thump something fierce.

When the man has disappeared around the corner and my heart is more or less back to normal, I wheel my bike up to the Masons' broken gate and push it open. A dog starts barking inside. A wooden crosspiece of the gate has rotted and collapsed so the bottom of the gate drags on the concrete path.

I lean my bike against the inside of the broken fence and lock it.

There's no bell or knocker on the front door. I rap with my knuckles. The barking dog scares me. It sounds like it's about to have itself a heart attack.

Then I realize I haven't got a clue what I'm going to say. I've got nothing prepared. Am I dumb or what!

A flap of curtain moves in the window. Before I can turn and run away, the porch light comes on and bolts and locks snap off and the door opens.

Mrs. Mason's face looks yellow under the dim porch light. She wears a light-colored shirt and a longish skirt — gray, I think, though it's hard to tell under the yellow light — and her dark hair is tied back in a ponytail. There's no veil now to hide her face.

She says nothing but seems to be looking at me like I'm something she discovered stuck to her shoe, like she knows I'm the one who stood by and let her son die.

The dog is growling at me and showing its teeth. The dog knows for sure.

Mrs. Mason looks past me into the street, turning her head to see both ways.

"Be quiet, Mango!" To me she says, "The dog won't bite you. Can I help you?"

"I'm Charley Callaghan."

There's no sign on her face that she recognizes my name. So maybe Benny didn't write it on the note he left.

She closes the door a bit, seems in a hurry to be rid of me. The dog stops growling but it doesn't take its eyes off me.

I gulp for air.

"I was a friend of Benny's."

"A friend of Benny's?"

I nod.

She stands looking at me for the longest time — for ages, it seems like. I'm just thinking I should say something quickly and go but then she steps back, holding the door open.

"Would you like to come in? I'm just putting Rico to bed."

I step inside.

Benny's kid brother comes running to the door, clutches his ma's leg and looks shyly up at me.

Now that she's inside with the door closed and locked, she seems more relaxed.

"Rico, this is a friend of Benny's."

"Hi, Rico. I'm Charley."

I follow them inside. The dog crouches beside his basket next to the sofa, watching me suspiciously.

There's no one else in the house.

Mrs. Mason says, "I'm about to read Rico a story. Please sit. I'll be only a few minutes."

"Look, Mrs. Mason, I just came by…"

Rico pulls at his ma's skirt and whispers to her.

She says to me, "Rico wants to know if you would like to see Pineapple's kittens."

Rico leads me shyly into the kitchen. In a dark corner beside the fridge there's a cardboard box with a cat and a bunch of kittens. The five kittens are a mixture of yellow, orange and brown.

Rico picks one up carefully in both hands, holding it up to show me. Its eyes are barely open.

Pineapple leaps out of the box and stalks around the kitchen making deep mewing sounds.

"You can pet it if you want," Rico says. I touch the kitten with a fingertip, keeping one eye on Pineapple.

"Rico loves Pineapple's kittens, don't you, Rico?" Mrs. Mason says.

I'm thinking that her voice sounds kind of phony bright, because her eyes stay dull and sad. It's like she's making an effort to sound cheerful.

We return to the other room. Mrs. Mason nods toward the sofa.

"Sit, why don't you? Say goodnight, Rico."

"G'night," says Rico.

"Goodnight, Rico."

I sit on the sofa and look about me. There isn't much to see. Easy chair, coffee table, telly, the usual stuff, except for a whole bunch of dolls. You'd never believe the dolls, dozens of them.

I get up and take one down off the shelf. It's made

out of papier mâché. They're on the mantel, on the stacks of books, on the telly — standing, sitting, lying, hanging. You name it, they're everywhere. There are gnomes with pointy hats and beards, pixies with grins as wide as their faces, elves, goblins, trolls, leprechauns and I don't know what all, painted in bright colors. Lots of them have oversized feet and hands, the big feet stuck right under a chin or chest. Cleverly made and painted they are, with sly expressions on their faces.

They're cool and funny. I can't help but grin as I look at them.

There's ugly-faced ones, too, like the ones on the outside of Dublin's St. Patrick's Cathedral — gargoyles, they're called — that stare down on you. They look like devils or evil spirits, with screaming gobs and lolling tongues; monsters with fangs or beaks, leering or howling. These little ones hang on Mrs. Mason's walls and sneer down at me and are not so funny.

I don't like them. The fact of the matter is, they're a bit scary.

I turn away and sit and wait in silence under the accusing stares of the gargoyles.

I catch the low murmur of Mrs. Mason's voice reading a story to Rico. I think about Benny and how he helped Annie pick up her stuff when she dropped her school bag, no easy thing if you ever saw all she carries in that thing — books and papers, loose coins, crayons, pens, pencils, sticky notes, paper clips, rubber bands and girl paraphernalia of all kinds, including a tiny blue wool doll Ma knitted for her when she was little. The doll's name is Prissy and goes everywhere with her.

I can picture Benny Mason crouching, picking up Annie's things for her.

Thinking of Annie reminds me that I should be getting back to Aunt Maeve's before someone misses me, but just then Mrs. Mason tiptoes out of the kid's bedroom, closing the door behind her softly.

"I'm making myself a pot of tea. Would you like some?"

"No, thanks. I should really be going."

"Would you like something else? Pop?"

"I should…"

She disappears into the kitchen.

It's weird sitting in Benny's living room looking at

all these trolls, dwarves and goblins. They don't look so funny any more. It's like they've come in from the woods and fields and mountains, out of their holes, gathering together in Benny's house to take a look at me, to see for themselves the kid who won the Nobel Prize for cowardice.

There, I've said the C word. Coward.

The gargoyles' twisted faces mock me.

We know you, Charley Callaghan and we know what you are.

I turn my eyes to the floor so I won't have to look at them.

"You're right, Charley. Turn your eyes away from the Little People lest they steal your soul."

I look up. Ma is standing near the door, all dressed up like she used to be in Dublin when she and Da were going out to dinner someplace: black dress, stockings, high heels, earrings, the works.

"Hi, Ma…you know I don't believe in all that Irish faeries nonsense."

"The best protection against the Little People, Charley, is a pure heart."

I remember the song:

The Moon hangs in the meadow
Where the Little People play.
If you happen to be passing
Then bow your head and pray.
Unless your heart be pure
They'll steal your soul away.

"Aw, come on, Ma. You don't believe all that blarney. Anyway, I don't have a pure heart. Far from it."

Ma says, "You're a good boy, Charley. And you take good care of Annie. Tell Annie —"

Before Ma can say any more, Mrs. Mason calls for me to come to the kitchen. Ma just smiles at me and waves and I go into the kitchen and me and Mrs. Mason sit facing each other at an old wooden table with a plate of coconut biscuits — cookies — between us.

The kitchen includes the eating area. It's big for such a small house. Next to a wall telephone there's a wooden table with a sewing machine and a chair with a cushion on it. If Mrs. Mason sits in the chair she'd be able to see out the window to the back yard, I reckon.

There are no trolls or elves in the kitchen except

for one gnome, the kind with the big hands and feet, sitting on the windowsill by the sewing machine.

On shelves near the window there's small jars of paint and varnish and glue. There's also dozens of spools of thread in every possible color.

Next to the spools of thread, in an alcove, there's a tightly crowded rack of clothing with tags attached, on hangers, and a second rack of tagged clothing behind the chair along the wall.

Mrs. Mason notices me looking.

"It's my workshop," she says. "I do sewing. Alterations mainly: skirts, dresses, trousers, the usual stuff."

And the dolls, I say to myself.

She lifts the lid and stirs the teapot.

"I work for several shops," she says. "They send me work they can't handle themselves, because they're too busy or the work is too difficult for them. Sometimes I make something for a special customer."

I need to tell her about Benny. Get it over with.

But I don't know how to start.

I sip my cola from the can, ignoring the glass.

"Look, Mrs. Mason…"

James Heneghan

"Call me Joanna, please."

"I'm real sorry about Benny," I finally say.

Her eyes fill with tears. "I know. Benny is…was lucky to have you as a friend."

Now. Tell her now. Give it to her straight.

But my tongue seems suddenly like it's made of foam rubber. I can't speak.

Her eyes glistening, she says, "How well did you know him?"

"Know Benny?" I'm thinking furiously, but my mind and tongue are disconnected. "He was in my English and Socials classes. We…"

But nothing comes. I sit in desperate silence.

Then I say, "Mrs. Mason — Joanna — I could take care of Rico for you anytime you need a babysitter. If you want. I've had lots of experience looking after my little sister."

"Thank you, Charles —"

"It's Charley."

"Charley. It's good of you to offer, but I don't leave the house much." She reaches for a Kleenex. "What is your sister's name? How old is she?"

I tell her.

"You must bring her round to meet Rico."

"I will." I worry about someone missing me. I swig back the remains of the can. "I've got to go. Thanks for the drink."

Joanna follows me to the door. "Be sure to come again. And bring your sister."

"I will," I say again.

"Goodnight, Charley. Thanks for coming." The bolts and chains rattle loudly as the door closes behind me. You wouldn't believe how many locks and chains she's got on that door.

I head home up the hill. I didn't tell Mrs. Mason what I went to tell her.

No courage. No backbone. Coward.

"Lucky to have you as a friend." The words play and replay in time with my furious pedaling.

4

While I was at the Mason house, Annie went into my room and I wasn't there. She didn't tell Aunt Maeve or Crazy Uncle Rufus, though, thank God. So I had to tell Annie where I was, which is why she wants to tag along this afternoon. Anyway, I promised Joanna I would bring her over for a visit. And this time, I vow to myself, I will tell Mrs. Mason the truth about me and Benny.

Mango starts with the barking even before I knock on the door. I can tell from the way she's taking it all in that Annie's eyes are not missing the rundown condition of the fence and front yard.

The door opens. Mango stops barking.

Mrs. Mason, smiling. "Hello, Charley. You've brought your sister. How nice. Come in, both of you."

Once inside, she says to Annie, "I'm Joanna. And I already know your name, Annie. Charley told me about you." Rico appears and clutches his ma's leg, same as before. "This is Rico."

"Hello, Rico."

"And this is Mango."

"Hi, Mango." Annie pats the dog.

"Come on in. Do you like chocolate chip cookies?" Mrs. Mason asks Annie. "They're homemade."

"Oh, yes." Annie smiles. "Chocolate's my favorite. I'd even eat spinach if it was dipped in chocolate. Charley said you've got kittens. Could I see them?"

"Of course. They're in the kitchen. Come on in."

"Mrs. Mason," I say, "could I call Aunt Maeve to let her know we're here?"

"Charley, you must call me Joanna. We're friends, right? There's a phone in the kitchen on the wall."

Aunt Maeve doesn't mind us staying. "So long as I know where you are," she says. "Home before dinner, okay?"

Annie loves Pineapple and her kittens. Then after a while she examines the trolls and goblins.

"Can I pick them up?" she asks Joanna.

"Of course, but be gentle with them. They break easily. And don't let the kittens near them."

"I won't," Annie promises. "I'll be very extra careful." She doesn't seem to mind the gargoyles.

Annie talks to Mango and plays with the dolls, having conversations with them, and lies on the floor among Rico's plastic toys and talks to the kittens. She asks Joanna if the dolls and the kittens have got names and when Joanna says no, she starts making up names for them, making Rico giggle.

Mrs. Mason and Annie like each other right away, I can tell, because Mrs. Mason talks to Annie about how she likes her hair and blah-blah-blah, typical girl stuff, back and forth. They talk together so much I don't get a chance for a private word with Mrs. Mason.

It turns out that the bedroom — Rico's and Benny's — has got lots of troll figures, too. They're sitting on bookshelves and the chest of drawers and on the bedside tables.

Also on the chest of drawers there's a framed picture of Benny with Mango. Benny is kneeling, Mango clasped to his chest.

As we leave, Joanna says, "Come whenever you can, okay? We love to see you, don't we, Rico? We don't get out to meet people very much."

Rico smiles and nods happily.

We stayed too long. Already it's beginning to get dark. Annie is dawdling. I grab the sleeve of her jacket to hurry her along.

There's a man walking over on the other side of the road, approaching us. I'm sure it's the scary guy again, the one with the black beard.

It's himself, all right. As he draws closer he stares across at us — or at Annie, more like, and then he turns quickly away into an alley so all I can see is his back retreating.

"Did you see that feller, Annie?"

"Yes, why?"

"No reason, except I don't like the look of him. Come on." I pull on her arm, hurrying her along even faster than before. "Let's move it, okay?"

Man with the black beard.

Blackbeard!

The air seems suddenly twenty degrees colder.

With Christmas only a month away the mall is busy at the weekend. I sweat like a marathon runner inside that stupid sausage suit. I'm terrible jaded when I get home, and I collapse into bed.

Sammy and Rebar are not at school. It's sure a relief not to have their ugly faces reminding me of Benny. Gossip says they've been suspended.

But I skip school on Wednesday and go to our own place and climb the stairs to Ma and Da's bedroom.

Bedroom closets in Maple Leaf Land are big — big enough for a game of football. I can stretch right out in them. Brilliant. I've got the doors open a tiny bit for air. Lights out.

I lie on the carpeted floor, Ma's sweaters, coats, shoes and dresses beside and above me. I breathe the faint familiar fragrances, not only of Ma but also of

Dublin — the River Liffey and the sands at Bray and the Guinness Brewery and Cleary's department store and cathedral incense and a whole stew of memories.

I begin to drift off to sleep.

"Wake up, Charley. You're mitching again."

"Aww! Ma! School is torture. And I'm terrible tired. And it's called skipping, not mitching."

I can't see her in the dark.

"School is what you make it, Charley, the same as life. And you shouldn't be in my closet." In the darkness her voice seems to come from the ceiling.

"I like it here, Ma. Besides, it's not your closet any more. I use it more than you so now it's mine."

"You'd be better riding your bike outside under the lovely trees, Charley."

"Leave me alone, Ma, I'm terrible jaded, okay? I only want to sleep."

"That job in the mall is taking too much out of you, Charley. Perhaps you should consider quitting the hotdog business. School is more imp—"

"I will, Ma, I will. I promise. Now if you could just let me sleep, okay?"

....

"Rico! Stay away from the gate," Joanna yells out the open window.

Rico and Annie are playing out back with Mango, throwing a rubber ball for him to fetch.

Joanna works at her sewing machine and keeps an eye on Rico. The back yard is enclosed with a high cedar hedge at the end and solid fences to the sides. The west fence, unlike the fence in the front yard, has a strong gate with a good high latch.

Rico sometimes tries to open the gate, usually when the ball or whatever he's using for Mango to fetch lands on the other side accidentally, but the latch always defeats him.

Joanna is angry. "I've told you to stay away!" she screams. "You're not to go near that gate, do you hear?"

My heart gives a jump. I can't believe Joanna screamed at Rico like that.

Rico cries.

It was Annie's idea to bring over a couple of board games — Snakes and Ladders and Monopoly — so we can teach Rico how to play. Rico likes Snakes and Ladders but Monopoly's a bit complicated for him.

He likes jigsaw puzzles, too. We rooted through our old stuff at home and found a few to take over.

Joanna likes it when we play with Rico, especially when she's busy with her sewing.

When it comes time to leave, Joanna, Rico and Mango come with us to the door.

"G'bye Mango," Annie says, kneeling to pet the dog.

Joanna smiles and scratches Mango behind his ears.

"Have you had Mango from a puppy?" Annie asks, looking up.

"Yes. Well, a big puppy. Benny found him. Rescued him, really."

"Rescued him?"

"Benny was on his bike, riding through the boatyard, you know? Near Waterfront Park? He saw a couple of boys at the end of the pier throw something into the water. This was when Benny was at his last school. The boys were laughing. Benny stopped and watched. Then he saw it was an animal, fighting to stay afloat in the waves. Benny waded into the water and pulled it out. It was a dog. Its legs, front and back, were tied. Would have drowned for sure. The two boys — high school age, Benny reckoned — started to run toward him, shouting and yelling, but he pushed the dog into his backpack, jumped on his bike and got away."

Annie is listening to this, eyes round like the bottoms of pop bottles, like she can't believe what she's hearing.

"His legs were tied!" She looks like she's about to explode.

Joanna nods. "With rope. Legs tied together front and back."

"But that's murder!"

"Kids can do awful things sometimes."

I'm thinking, *Tell me about it.*

"That was very brave of Benny," says Annie. She turns to Mango and kisses the animal near to death.

"So of course you had to keep Mango after that, huh?" I say.

"I needed a good guard dog anyway," says Joanna. "Benny named him Mango because of his color. He's a yellow Labrador, the vet told me."

"Isn't he kind of small for a Lab?" I say, thinking

that medium-sized, sharp-toothed Mango looks more like a terrier-spaniel cross, with maybe a pinch of piranha thrown in.

Joanna shrugs. "He barks and growls if anyone comes near the house, so I guess he's a good enough guard dog. Benny loved that dog." Her eyes grow damp.

"Thanks, guys," she says as we're leaving. "You're a great help. I don't know what I'd do without you."

On the way home Annie says, "Benny was a hero saving Mango like that."

I don't say anything.

6

I start doing small chores for Joanna, like helping keep the living room tidy by putting things like cushions and books back in their places if Rico or Annie leave them lying about, rinsing glasses and cups in the kitchen, stuff like that.

I make myself useful, in other words.

I say, "I'll take out the garbage, okay?"

"Thanks, Charley. I'll hold the door open for you," says Joanna.

Joanna unfastens the bolts and chains. There are four of them, two up and two down, plus the catch in the middle. Then she waits at the door and watches me dump the garbage in the different bins.

"No need to wait," I shout back at her. "I'll take care of the bolts when I come back."

"No problem, Charley. I don't mind."

It takes me a minute to do the job. Joanna waits. Then when I go back inside she shoots the bolts home. Maybe she thinks I'll forget to lock the door behind me.

On Saturday I ride my bike over to Joanna's and she asks me to pick up a few things at the Safeway, which I do, pretending as I go that I'm Lance Armstrong in my yellow jersey, tearing down the far side of the Alpe d'Huez. Whooosh!

Later, while I'm taking Joanna's garbage out to the bin I take a good look at the state of the front yard. It's terrible scruffy. Nothing's been done outside for years it looks like.

It's too late in the year to do much more than a clean-up. In the spring I could try and help Joanna put in a flower or vegetable garden, or grass if that's what she wants. And maybe I could try and figure out how to fix the sagging front gate.

"I could clean up the weeds and stuff in the front yard, if you like," I say to her.

"Thanks, Charley. That's very kind of you. Every time I look at it I'm ashamed what the neighbors must think. There's a machete for chopping the long grass in the shed out back, and there's other tools, too, a shovel and a rake, and work gloves if you need them. You won't cut yourself, will you?"

I pull a face and she laughs.

I don't care about getting my hands dirty, so I don't bother with the gloves.

"You won't mind if I lock you out? I like to keep the door locked. Just hammer on the door if you need anything."

I start chopping the thistles and weeds and grass with the machete. I'm thinking about Joanna and her locks and bolts.

Some women are pretty nervous, I guess, especially if they're single with a small kid. Or they might've had a bad experience with someone breaking in.

I grab the tops of the withered stalks and grass in one hand and then I bend and chop as close to the ground as I can, throwing the weeds behind me as I go.

The thistles prove to be a bit of a problem because even though they're dead and withered they're still spiky and sharp. I decide to use just one glove, on my left hand.

It's hard work. And slow. I thought it'd be a lot easier somehow.

After almost an hour only half of the yard is cleared. And there's red, angry blisters on my right hand, between my thumb and forefinger.

I try reversing things so that I grab the stalks with my right hand and chop with my left, but it's awkward and slow.

I miss and hit myself on the shin with the machete. "Ouch!" I drop the machete. That hurt. I pull up the leg of my jeans: broken skin but not really any bleeding.

I should stop and finish the job some other day but I push on.

The second half takes longer than an hour. By the time I'm finished it's not only my shin that's aching, it's also my right shoulder and wrist from swinging the machete. My hands, too, are destroyed with blisters. I've got barely enough energy to stuff all the cuttings into plastic bags and twist-tie the tops.

I stack the bags along the fence to be taken away by the city workers. There are eleven black garbage bags, packed tight with weeds.

Phew! I can't believe it was such a hard job.

If you're wondering what the front yard looks like

when I'm through with it, well, I've got to admit it still looks pretty scruffy, like it's had a bad haircut.

Joanna is chuffed, though.

"It's much tidier, Charley, and looks cared for. You did a great job. Thanks. Now come in and have a bite to eat before you go."

"No, thanks. I got to go. It's Saturday. I'm on duty in an hour. Probably drop in again tomorrow."

I don't let her see my hands.

••••

Twenty-five shopping days to Christmas. The mall is so crowded I can hardly move. Which is good because I don't have to dance so much. Even if I could. And I can't because I'm so aching and sore from the yard work.

I thought of calling in sick but I don't because Harvey would have a hard time finding someone to fill in at such short notice.

So I climb into my hotdog suit, trying not to think of my aches and blisters.

Right away I'm in trouble. A little brat of a kid, seven or eight years old, starts pestering me, following me about and yelling things like, "I can see you in there. You don't fool me," and, "You know what kinda junk they put inside hotdogs? You ever hear of Mad Cow Disease, huh?" On and on. I can't get rid of him.

I must use one or two bad words because his mother complains to Harvey and you know what? Now I'm out of a job.

"That's it! I've had it with you, Irish. Don't bother asking for a reference."

And that's the end of my short career in show business.

Ma will be pleased.

7

On Sunday Annie gets her nose stuck in Joanna's sewing corner, watching Joanna sewing, examining the colored spools of thread, running her fingers through the materials. Joanna shows her how to use the sewing machine and does other things, too, like fixing Annie's hair and talking with her about girl stuff like shoes and clothes.

In just a week and a half it's like me and Annie have become part of the family. Even growly Mango doesn't growl any more when we knock on the door, and Pineapple doesn't even open her eyes when we pick up her kittens.

It's hard sometimes for me to get Annie to leave and go home.

....

It's the first day of December. Joanna's place after school. While Annie sews a white zig-zag pattern around a piece of red material, I take out the garbage, clean up the kitchen and change the litter in Pineapple's box.

Then, because it's starting to get dark, I say, "Time to go, Annie."

"Just let me finish this." She's working at the sewing machine.

"If we don't go now it'll be dark, so move it."

"One minute, that's all it'll take me. One minute, so hold your horses, Charley!"

Hold your horses. That's what Ma used to say.

The dog always comes to the door with Joanna and Rico to see us off.

Annie kisses Mango and Mango licks her face.

"You're not supposed to kiss dogs, you know," I say as we head home. "You could catch something horrible and deadly."

"Oh, yeah? Like what?"

"I dunno, rabies or…"

"Rabies is only if a rabid dog bites you."

"Well, how do you know Mango hasn't got rabies?"

"Because I know, that's why. Gee, you're so stupid sometimes, Charley, really!"

She's only eight but she sounds like she's eighteen most of the time. I don't know how she knows all the stuff she knows.

I would never admit this to anyone, but sometimes I think girls are smarter than boys.

At dinner that night Da says, "Your aunt tells me that you and Annie are spending a lot of time over at the Mason place."

I feel my face get red. "Aunt Maeve said it's okay for us to go after school."

"But almost every day, Charley? What's going on?"

"Nothing's going on. Mrs. Mason could use some help, that's all."

"And you and Annie are helping?"

"Yes. I work around her yard sometimes, run errands, and Annie plays with her little kid while Mrs. Mason catches up on her sewing, stuff like that. And Mrs. Mason is teaching her how to sew on her machine."

"Maybe your Aunt Maeve could use a little help over at her place. Do you ever think of that? Your uncle doesn't do much around the house except make a mess with his kites."

"We do help Aunt Maeve. We have chores."

"And you're still taking care of your sister? You pick her up after school every day and make sure she gets home okay? You're watching out for her?"

"Of course, Da." I feel good about that. I've never missed picking her up, even on the days I skip out of school.

"You're the man of the family when I'm not here, Charley, you know that. Get home before dark. No later, okay? I rely on you."

"Okay, Da." I mean it. He can rely on me.

He's right about Crazy Uncle Rufus, though. Did I mention that Crazy Uncle Rufus builds kites? And flies them at Waterfront Park on windy days? Anyway, he does, and he makes a mess in the dining room with glue and paper and scraps of materials and hardly ever puts his tools away and poor old Aunt Maeve always has to clean up after him. The kites he makes are pretty good, though. He makes all shapes — deltas and boxes and diamonds and other kinds I don't remember the names of.

He took me kite flying with him one windy

Saturday afternoon — this was before Ma was sick in hospital — and I watched him running about the field like a maniac. The kite flew straight up into the sky, so high I could hardly see it.

"Look at her soar, Charley," he yelled. "She flies straight to heaven."

He passed the line over to me and let me hold it. It was like trying to control a runaway horse, the pull on my arms and wrists so fierce.

"Follow your bliss, Charley," yelled Crazy Uncle Rufus, his face red with excitement.

I was afraid the line would be torn from my hands, and Crazy Uncle Rufus's kite would be lost. Then the line suddenly slackened and the kite began losing height.

"Keep her aloft, Charley!" yelled Crazy Uncle Rufus.

But I couldn't. I didn't know how.

Crazy Uncle Rufus grabbed the line from my hands and began a wild dance, whooping and laughing and waving his arms about and soon the kite was soaring again.

"Kites rise highest *against* the wind, Charley, not *with* it," he yelled.

"Ah, ye did well for a beginner, Charley," Crazy Uncle Rufus said afterwards, when we were driving home. "But kite-flying is an ancient Irish art, and it helps a lot if ye have the blessing of the Little People."

I think what Crazy Uncle Rufus really meant was if I want to be a good kite flyer like him, then I need to be crazy like him.

••••

I decide we'll stay no longer than an hour if we go to Joanna's on weekdays. I think of Blackbeard. It's not as safe on the streets after the sun sets, and you hear so much about creeps who go after little kids, especially girls. I didn't like the look he gave Annie the other day. I get the heebies just thinking about it.

The next morning I take a long carving knife from the drawer and slip it into my school bag.

"What's with the knife in the school bag, Charley?"

"It's to protect Annie, Ma."

"Taking a knife to school isn't such a good idea, Charley. You know that."

Ma looks like she's just come out of the shower — flushed face, hair in a towel, white terrycloth bathrobe, slippers.

I drop the knife back into the drawer. Then I see the potato peeler with its sharp end.

"What about this, Ma?" I say, turning from the drawer, but she's gone.

I feel the end of the peeler with the edge of my thumb. Useful for sharpening pencils, if anyone asks.

But could I really use it? Could I strike out with it, like a sword or dagger, and draw somebody's blood?

I toss it into my school bag. If Blackbeard tries anything, sure as Helsinki he's going to get it right in the place where he keeps his valuables, if you know what I mean.

I'll show him I'm no coward.

8

Annie can't wait to get over to Joanna's after school every day for Joanna to teach her how to make napkins and place mats on the sewing machine.

I watch them with their heads together, bent over the kitchen table or sitting side by side at the sewing machine, Annie happy and worry free, almost the way she used to be before Ma died, when she had lots of energy and way too much to say. Anyone with a pair of eyes can see that coming to the Mason place is good for her.

Did I mention about all the rain we've been getting? We had a long dry summer, but Vancouver's a wet place in the winter, Aunt Maeve says, and over here on the north shore at the foot of the mountains, it's even wetter.

You'd think it being December there'd be snow,

but no way, just rain. There's tons of snow on the mountains for the skiers and snowboarders, but down here closer to sea level we're socked in by a dark belly of wet cloud, and it gets dark real early.

Every morning, before setting out for school, I get in the habit of taking my sword — the spud peeler — from my school bag and slipping it down the sock of my right leg.

I know I can get to it fast if I need to. I've been practicing. I'm quick on the draw.

On Friday, Rico is stretched out on the living-room floor flipping through the pages of a picture book.

"What you got there, Rico?" Annie sits beside him. "A new book?"

"It's called *Big Bill*," says Rico. "Will you read it to me?"

Annie hunkers down beside him and reads the book to him.

I leave her to it and take care of the garbage while Joanna stands guard at the door as usual. Then I jog over to the corner grocery and pick up a carton of milk.

When I get back, Annie is sitting at the sewing machine with Joanna, and Rico is still on the floor looking through the pictures of his new book.

I put the milk in the fridge and then sit at the kitchen table. Joanna has left orange juice and granola bars out for a snack.

Rico comes and sits down beside me.

"Will you read *Big Bill* to me, Charley?"

"Sure, Rico."

Annie says, "Joanna, do you think you could teach me how to make those gnomes with big hands and feet? I love them."

Joanna says, "Me, too. But I don't know how to make them, Annie."

"You didn't make the trolls and gnomes?" says Annie.

"Me? No. Benny made them."

"You're not reading." Rico is becoming impatient with me. I'm not paying enough attention to his book.

Annie says, "Benny made everything?"

"That's right, Annie."

My head jerks up from Rico's book, and I stare at Joanna.

Benny made everything. I had no idea.

The gnome on Joanna's windowsill is looking at me, its face sad with disappointment and reproach.

....

"Aunt Maeve, what's it called when someone is too scared to leave their house?"

"Claustrophobia? No, agoraphobia, I think. Look it up. Do you know someone like that, Charley?"

"Maybe. I'm not sure."

Benny's death is always on my mind. It doesn't get smaller, it gets bigger and bigger. It's like a house filling up with furniture. My mind is crammed with Benny's furniture and it's getting harder and harder to move around. I keep barking my shins and bruising my elbows on the tables and chairs, keep knocking into the sneering gargoyles and disappointed gnomes.

I still can't tell Joanna, and the longer I leave it the harder it gets. But I can't keep the black secret all to myself, it's too big.

The whole thing is like a bomb inside me, ticking away, waiting to explode.

"Hi."

It's Danny Whelan from my English class. He's wearing earphones around his neck.

"Hi." I nod back at him.

"Okay to sit here?"

"You bet." Another North American phrase I picked up. You bet.

He sits opposite me at the cafeteria table and opens his lunch bag.

"Whelan's an Irish name," I say.

He nods. "Ancestor came to Montreal way back during the Great Irish Famine of 1848."

"What place in Ireland?"

He shrugs. "No idea. Place with a bunch of lakes, I think."

"Killarney, maybe."

"Maybe."

He asks me a few questions about what music I like. We talk.

When lunch is over he says, "Catch you later."

"You bet."

Catch you later. I like that. I add it to my growing list of Canadian.

Catch you later. You bet.

....

"Look! It's that man again," says Annie.

We've just arrived at Joanna's after school.

Annie's right. Blackbeard is standing in a neighbor's unfenced front yard across the street, a few lots away from Joanna's house.

"Pretend you haven't seen him, Annie."

I know it's himself even in the gloom of the mountain shadows. He is big and dark, and almost blends in with the purple light in the neighbor's yard.

It's obvious he's trying to hide because he ducks behind a bush when he sees us.

It's the first time I've seen him in daytime. In the gloom he looks even scarier than at night. It isn't just the beard. It's also his huge size and the hungry glare in his dark eyes.

He seems to be staring straight at Annie.

I knock on Joanna's door and she lets us in. Before

the door closes I look back over at the neighbor's yard, but Blackbeard has disappeared.

••••

A few days later we see Blackbeard again after school. He's passing the corner grocery a couple of blocks from Joanna's.

My heart pounds with fear as I bend over and feel the shape of the spud peeler in my sock. I like the feel of it next to my leg.

I pretend to tie my shoelace while Annie waits.

When I stand up and look around, Blackbeard has gone.

If Blackbeard is the kind who kidnaps kids, shouldn't he have a car, luring his victims inside with candy or asking for help to find a lost puppy? Even Annie might go with him if he did that. Seeing him so often can't be coincidence.

Is Blackbeard planning to kidnap Annie?

A chill strikes through to my belly.

Suddenly my spud peeler seems like no weapon at all.

9

It comes without warning. Even Mango is caught napping.

Joanna and Annie are at the sewing machine and me and Rico are working on a puzzle at the kitchen table when he comes crashing through the back door into the kitchen like a bomb. The locks shatter and the door splinters into pieces.

Blackbeard!

Mango rushes in, snarling and growling like a lion.

"Arrgrrrgh!"

It seems like everyone's screaming. Annie falls to the floor, her hands clasped to her ears in fright.

"Charley!" she shrieks. I rush over to her.

Joanna leaps to her feet, screaming.

Blackbeard roars at her and plunges toward Rico.

Mango launches himself at Blackbeard's leg, snarling and growling.

Joanna is like a madwoman. She screams and grabs Blackbeard, trying to pull him back out the shattered door.

"Yaaa!" yells Blackbeard, shaking her off.

Joanna launches herself at the kitchen counter, reaching for a long knife. She doesn't make it. Blackbeard throws her away roughly. The knife clatters to the floor and she collides with the stacked dishes on the drainboard. The dishes are swept to the floor in an almighty crash and Joanna goes down with them, striking her head on the edge of counter and lying still.

Rico screams and runs to his ma's side. Joanna doesn't move when he pulls at her, trying to wake her.

Blackbeard swings his leg quickly, kicking high to shake off the dog. Mango flies off the leg, taking a scrap of Blackbeard's trousers with him. He hits the wall with a thud and falls to the floor.

I'm in a state of shock. I can't move, watching helplessly as Blackbeard lunges at Rico.

Annie screams, "Charley!"

Blackbeard trips over Pineapple, who is streaking

across the floor to protect her kittens. He yells something foreign and falls to the floor with a crash.

Mango rushes in again, snarling and growling as he fights to tear the ear from Blackbeard's head. The man bellows with pain and anger, beats Mango off and staggers to his feet, clutching the side of his head. Blood pours down the side of his face and neck.

I stare at the blood, and then I come to life. I throw myself at Blackbeard and kick his shins as fast and hard as I can — twice, once with each foot. But I'm like a fly attacking a gorilla. I try to get in close so I can deliver a Dublin kiss but it's impossible because he's way too big and is moving too fast for me, and besides, I've never done one before. He reaches for Rico who is clinging to his ma's limp arm. He tears Rico away from his ma, but Rico, wriggling and screaming, slips from his grasp and falls to the floor.

"Momma! Momma!" he screams.

As Blackbeard reaches again for Rico, Mango launches himself at Blackbeard and sinks his teeth into his leg. Blackbeard yells and falls backwards, and something rattles and falls to the floor.

Car keys. Blackbeard's car.

I bend quickly and grab them and hurl them as hard as I can out the broken door into the back yard, yelling to Annie and Rico at the same time, "Lock yourselves in the bathroom!"

Rico tries to go to his ma but Annie throws her arms about him and half lifts, half drags Rico out of the kitchen.

Blackbeard is like a madman. He charges out into the back yard to search for his keys. Mango chases after him.

Joanna stirs feebly on the floor.

I run to the wall telephone. With trembling fingers I punch the 911 emergency number.

"Come quick!" I yell into the phone. "Police and ambulance!" I'm shaking. "Eighteen-eighty-eight Acorn Street. Come quick! Kidnap! Robbery! Come quick!"

Mango bursts into the kitchen from the back yard, Blackbeard's car keys in his jaws.

Stupid dog!

I'm still holding the phone when Blackbeard comes thumping along fast behind Mango. He sees the phone in my hand and grabs it and pulls, ripping the cord from the wall. He hurls the phone at Mango and grabs the keys from his jaws.

Mango sinks his teeth into Blackbeard's ankle again and hangs on.

He rips Mango off his ankle by grasping him by the collar in one big hand and cutting off his air. Mango releases his hold. Blackbeard hurls him at the wall.

"Aaarrgh!"

I go to kick him but he swats me with the back of his hand. "Hup!"

I go flying, crashing into the table and falling to the floor. Mango whimpers with pain, trying to stand.

Blackbeard runs to the bathroom, smashes open the locked door, sweeps Rico up and comes running, almost tripping over himself in his haste, back toward the kitchen, Rico tucked under one arm.

Mango isn't finished yet. With the last of his strength he comes at Blackbeard again, gluing himself to his leg.

Blackbeard heads for the shattered kitchen door, trying to make his escape, dragging Mango along with him.

Payback

I stagger up from the floor. My jaw feels broken and my back has surely snapped in half.

My sword! I forgot about my spud peeler! I reach down and pull it from my sock and block Blackbeard's path, pointing the blade at him.

But he just keeps coming, waves me out of the way and bashes me on the shoulder with the hard edge of his meaty hand.

I stab at the giant's thigh as I go down, but I pierce his out-flung hand instead. The peeler skitters off along the floor. Blackbeard drops Rico and the car keys.

I painfully snatch the car keys off the floor, stagger into the bathroom through the smashed door, hurl the keys down the toilet and reach for the lever to flush them away. Blackbeard grabs me from behind and pulls. I shoot backwards into the hallway and hit the wall.

I try to get up but my legs won't support me. I see Blackbeard plunge his hand into the toilet and grab the keys.

Then, with the keys in his hand, he runs and drags a screaming Rico from behind the living-room sofa, where he and Annie are trying to hide. He makes for the kitchen door, Rico under his arm, wriggling and yelling, "Momma! Momma!"

And then the police are suddenly there, bursting into the kitchen — four cops with guns drawn.

"Police! Hold it right there!"

"Back against the wall!"

"Put the kid down nice and easy!"

Blackbeard takes one look at them and gives up. He releases Rico and slumps to the floor, back against the kitchen cupboards, all the fight gone out of him. A policeman slips handcuffs onto his wrists, ignoring the blood.

Rico runs to his ma, who is barely conscious.

"Momma!"

I stagger to my knees, groggy with pain. Annie comes out from behind the sofa and throws her arms around me and I fall again, taking Annie down with me.

"Charley!" she cries. I lean my back against the wall, sucking air.

Two ambulance men arrive. The kitchen is crowded. They start strapping Joanna onto a stretcher.

"You'll be all right, ma'am. Just you relax now."

One of the ambulance men turns and looks at me.

"Stay where you are, son, and don't move, okay?"

Which is fine with me. I don't want to move. Ever.

Annie crouches down beside me and takes my hand. She's got a bloody swelling on her forehead.

The ambulance man takes a good look at me and Annie, who keeps holding my hand. Then he takes a look at Blackbeard's bleeding wounds while a police-man stands over them. Rico kneels beside his ma's stretcher, trembling with fright, staring over at the man who came to take him away.

The kitchen is quiet.

Blackbeard, sitting slumped on the kitchen floor, back against the cupboards, stares at the boy.

"My little Rico," he groans softly.

His dark eyes are swimming with tears.

10

All I remember about the hospital is white-coated figures fussing over me while I worry if Annie is okay.

The next thing is I'm home at Aunt Maeve's.

In bed. In the dark.

I know it's Aunt Maeve's because of the nightlight in the Blessed Virgin holy water font. Every time I wake up I see the orange light and shadows flickering on the wall and ceiling, and Ma watching over me.

The next morning I slide out of bed. My legs are so weak I can hardly stand. Takes me ages to get to the bathroom.

The mirror shows me a Frankenstein monster.

I look deadly. I'm shocked. My left eye is completely closed and there's black-and-blue swellings all over my mug, including my lip. My face is a different shape altogether, like the map of Ireland.

"Oh, Charley!" says Annie, coming in behind me. "Aunt Maeve says you must stay in bed today."

"I'm fine."

She grabs me by the wrist and walks me back to bed.

I'm not fine. The bed looks grand. All I want to do is sleep.

I climb in and Annie pulls up the covers and then leans over me, whispering, "Will I bring you some ice cream? Aunt Maeve bought a new carton. It's your favorite — chocolate pecan."

I must have gone off because I don't remember eating any ice cream.

Annie and Aunt Maeve are there when I wake up. I close my eyes again. Then it's just Annie there. I notice the swelling on her forehead.

"How's your head, Annie?"

"It's nothing. Just a bump. Would you like me to read to you? I could read whatever book you want. Or your bike magazine?"

"I think I'll just close my eyes again for a few minutes, Annie."

I stay in bed for the rest of the day. Annie keeps popping in and out keeping me company and driving me crazy, bringing books and food and board games.

Joanna telephones. Aunt Maeve brings the phone into the bedroom.

"I called to thank you for what you did, Charley. For saving Rico. I owe you more than I can ever repay."

My jaw feels stiff. I can hardly speak.

"Look, Joanna...I've got to talk to you, okay?" It's an effort. "Tomorrow. I'll be there in the morning."

I don't get up until the afternoon.

I call Joanna and then walk over. I don't trust myself on my bike.

I take my time because I'm terrible stiff. It's Sunday and the street is quiet.

I knock on the door. No barking Mango.

Joanna lets me in. The side of her face is all bruised, and she's got a black eye.

When she sees my face she says, "Oh, Charley!" Her eyes round as Frisbees. "I'm so sorry!" Big hug.

I just go limp, arms by my sides while she moans over me.

"I'm okay. How's Rico?"

"Rico is fine. Hardly a bruise on him, thank heaven."

I follow her into the living room but she keeps looking at me, horrified.

I don't see the cats anywhere.

Rico comes running and throws his arms around my legs. I try to lift him up but quickly put him down again because my back and arms and shoulders are wrecked.

The gnomes and trolls and gargoyles and all the rest know why I'm here. I can tell by the looks on their faces, leering and jeering at my misery and guilt.

And why shouldn't they? They are Benny's creatures, after all.

I follow Joanna into the kitchen. The first thing I see is the smashed door. I think of Blackbeard coming through it like a tank.

I ease myself into a chair. Joanna has been cleaning up, but the kitchen is still a mess. One of the lower cupboard doors is missing.

"Where's the table? And two chairs are missing."

"The legs are broken. I put them outside in the back." She hands me a can of pop from the fridge, and a glass. Rico returns to his jigsaw puzzle in the living room.

"Where's Mango?"

"At the vet's. He'll be okay." She sits.

"He's the number one grandest guard dog. You should've seen him. Ferocious. Kept rushing in. Tore half of the guy's ear off." I don't tell her about the keys.

She nods. "He's a wonderful dog, all right."

I look around.

"What about Pineapple and her kittens? Are they okay?"

"Yes. She's moved them to a new spot — under my bed."

"I don't see your sewing machine."

"It fell and broke. I can get it repaired. It shouldn't be a problem. But I can't stop looking at your poor face, Charley. I'm so angry at —"

"Rico's father."

"Yes."

"What will happen to him?"

"I don't know. The police and the immigration office will decide. They'll deport him, I hope." She

shrugs. "If you hadn't stopped him yesterday..."
Tears flood her eyes. "I have so much to thank you
for, Charley."

I shake my head. "No, you don't. I —"

This is it. I've got to tell her. I take a sip of pop.
Then I clear my throat.

"Joanna, there's something I've got to tell you,
something you don't know about me. I tried to tell
you that very first day but —"

She reaches out a hand and places it over mine.

"There's no need, Charley." She sighs. "I already
know."

"You already know?"

"Yes, Charley."

"You know I wasn't Benny's friend?"

She shakes her head. "Benny had no friends. If he
had he would have told me. Besides, a friend would
have helped him."

My heart is crushed at her words. But she's right.
Benny didn't get any help from me.

She knew all the time and never said anything!

"So why did you let me keep coming here?"

"I saw your pain, Charley. That's all. I couldn't
turn you away."

I thought I was helping her but she was helping me? Is that what she's saying?

"I didn't stand up for him. I just watched."

"Don't blame yourself, Charley. I'm the one. It was my entire fault. I'm more to blame for poor Benny's death than anyone."

"What do you mean?"

The words flood out of her.

"I pushed him to go to school, to face up to his problems, to be responsible, to be a man, but I should have protected him. I'm his mother. I thought I was doing what was best for him, but I should have known. The evidence was under my nose all the time but I couldn't see it. So much time sleeping. He wasn't reading, and he stopped making his gnomes and elves, kept to his room, wouldn't eat —"

By now she's sobbing, and I feel my eyes prickle as I watch her.

"I could have kept him home," she says to me, her voice flat. "I could have kept him safe. I will never forgive myself. Not in a thousand years will I ever forgive myself."

11

Da gets home early in the afternoon.

When he sees me his jaw drops.

He already knows about me and Annie being in the hospital. Aunt Maeve told him last night on the phone.

"You look terrible!" he says. His face looks like there's a vacuum inside his skull sucking the skin tight around his cheekbones.

"I know, but I'm okay."

Aunt Maeve comes over to our house and tells Da the story again, this time with my help. You wouldn't believe the number of questions my da asks.

When it's over, Da says, "You're a brave boy, Charley. But I don't approve of you putting yourself in harm's way. It's not a dead hero I want for a son, you hear me? I still don't quite understand why you and Annie were over at the Mason place so much —

yes, I know you told me how you were trying to help, but it doesn't quite add up. I'd like to meet that woman myself."

Now I've got to tell my da the truth.

I take a deep breath and give it to him straight, tell him the whole story, my part in Benny Mason's death, how I could've stuck up for Benny but didn't.

Telling Da is hard. But telling Joanna was harder.

"I'm one of the reasons Benny killed himself. When the others were slagging him I stood by and let it happen. I should have said something. It's like I helped kill him."

After Da has heard everything, he says, "Life is about choices, Charley. What you did was wrong, saying nothing. You made the wrong choice. But Benny Mason's wrong choices were fatal. He could have asked for help from his mother or from the school. Instead, he chose to jump off a bridge to his death. He chose the wrong way to solve his problem."

I tell Da about the fire alarms.

Da says, "It's a pity no one was listening. Look, I admire you for taking responsibility, Charley, but you can't pay for Benny's wrong choices. It's over. It's finished. You helped the boy's ma. You tried to make amends. You're a grand boy, Charley. I'm proud of you. And if your ma was here she'd be proud of you, too."

He reaches out and gives my shoulder a squeeze.

"Now you've got to put it behind you and move on, you understand?"

Seems to me moving on won't be as easy as it sounds. For starters, I'll never forget Benny Mason.

....

Me and Annie drive with Da over to the Mason place in the late afternoon.

Joanna and Da shake hands and then Joanna introduces Rico, who is holding one of Pineapple's kittens. Mango is back home in his basket, but he isn't well enough for his barking routine at the front door.

Annie kneels on the floor and baby-talks him.

"Is the brave Mango home again where he belongs?" She nuzzles the dog's ruff and Mango's tail twitches feebly as he flicks a couple of jaded licks at Annie's face.

"I'm sorry for your loss," Da says to Joanna. "I didn't know Benny but I hear he was a fine boy."

Joanna smiles. "Please come in and sit down."

Me and Annie and Rico stay and talk to Mango. Da and Joanna head into the kitchen.

I scratch Mango's silky ear and he pushes his nose into my hand.

"You did a grand job, Mango. You went after that feller something fierce. I'll never forget the way you kept coming back at him. Me and Annie and Rico are going to make you a special medal."

"That's a lovely idea," says Annie. "Isn't it, Rico?"

Rico's not sure what a medal is but he grins and nods.

I hear Da say in the kitchen, "Do you mind if I ask you a few questions about this man who attacked my son?"

I move closer to the kitchen door.

"His name is Carlos Escobar. He is Rico's father. I met him many years ago, here in North Vancouver. I was alone. Benny's father had been killed in an accident. Benny was quite small when I met Carlos. Then I had Rico. Very soon after that, Carlos left Canada. He didn't like it here and wanted to go back to his own country.

"Carlos asked me to go with him, but I didn't

want that. He is a good man — he means well and has a kind heart — but Benny and I could never live with his uncontrollable rages. Besides, Carlos and Benny did not get along. Carlos wrote me many times asking me to bring just Rico with me. We could have a good life together, he said. But I didn't answer his letters. His last letter threatened to come and take Rico away from me if I did not do as he asked. Then the letters stopped. I heard nothing more from him."

"Until now."

"Yes. I knew he would never give up his son, and that he would come back for him one day. So I moved and changed my name to Mason, my mother's name before she married. My mistake was staying in North Vancouver. I should have moved to a place far away where he could never find me."

A long silence follows. Then she speaks again.

"If he had taken Rico away I would have lost both my sons. And that would be the end of me."

12

Early the next morning Da goes up to his and Ma's room and starts emptying Ma's closet of coats, sweaters, shirts, skirts, dresses and shoes — everything — into boxes.

I know what he's doing because he's left the bedroom door open and I'm not blind. I can see the pile of empty cardboard liquor store boxes stacked against the wall.

"What are you doing, Da?"

He stops and looks at me. "It's time to move on, Charley. I'm taking your mother's things over to the Salvation Army tomorrow. There's lots of poor people can use them. Want to give me a hand?"

"Does Annie know you're doing this?"

"She knows. She's keeping a few things."

I start helping, packing clothing into boxes. I

decide to keep one of her sweaters, the black and gray one. The smell of Ma hasn't faded a bit.

"Let it all go, Charley."

It's Ma, leaning against the wall near the double mirrored doors of her closet, watching Da moving back and forth, his arms full of clothes. She's wearing her Dublin grubs: faded pink T-shirt, baggy gray sweatpants, slippers. She looks the way she looked when she was working in our old kitchen, before we came to Canada.

"Aw, Ma. I hate to see all your stuff going."

"I know, Charley. But your da's right. It's time for you to move on. There's a whole life waiting for you to live." She smiles and waves a hand at the boxes and the sweater I'm holding in my hands. "So let everything go, okay?"

"I don't know, Ma. Things won't be the same."

"Nothing ever stays the same, Charley."

"I know, Ma. It's just that your sweaters and stuff made me feel like you're here with me."

"I am always here with you, Charley."

I look at her. Then I drop her sweater into a box.

"Goodbye, Charley."

My throat is so swollen I can hardly say it.

"Goodbye, Ma."

"That just about does it," says Da from inside the closet, empty except for Annie's keepers.

I walk in and take one last lungful of air. It's a big deep one — a last breath to keep for the rest of my life.

Then we leave and I close the doors.

••••

Da went to work this morning, back to the island, and me and Annie are skipping school at Aunt Maeve's. Da said it was okay. He called the two schools, explaining our absence. We're still recovering from Friday's madness. Crazy Uncle Rufus is taking a day off work so he can be with us.

The sky is black and the rain is coming down so hard I can hear it hissing in the gutters, drumming on the roof, drumming on my head.

Aunt Maeve and Annie watch from the kitchen window.

"How will I know I'm done, Uncle Rufus?" I shout over the noise of the rain.

Crazy Uncle Rufus doesn't answer. He just smiles.

Me and Crazy Uncle Rufus are standing in the back yard in our underpants. I can feel the grass between my toes and the rain on my skin and on my bruised face, head, shoulders, chest, and I'm looking up at the black sky with my eyes closed, tasting the lashing rain on my tongue and swollen lip.

It's cold out here but it feels good.

We stand in the back yard for a long time.

Until we're done.

Then Crazy Uncle Rufus gives me a wink, and we go inside.

....

At school the other kids see my mess of a face, but they don't say very much except stuff like, "What does the other guy look like?"

Only a few more days left before the Christmas vacation.

Dill Pickles is preparing us for a new unit starting after Christmas. She's working with our science teachers and having us sign up for Save Our Planet projects. We can work in pairs if we want.

Could be interesting. We'll get class time in the library for research and we can pick a topic like ecology, acid rain, climate change, ancient forests, whales, genetic engineering and a bunch of stuff like that. The topics and project guide are listed on the overhead and I'm copying them into my notebook.

When the bell goes at the end of the period, I've pretty well made up my mind to do something on Pacific rainforests, because I love all the trees here.

I close my notebook, but I feel like I forgot something.

I open the book again and stare at the pages of notes. They seem okay. Date assignment due, format — video, essay, story, drama or other presentation — length, margins. The usual stuff. I haven't forgotten anything.

Then I notice there are no screaming heads.

. . . .

At lunch time in the cafeteria I find myself a vacant table. I don't want to talk to anyone. But Danny Whelan ambles over and sits opposite.

He opens up his lunch bag.

"You got a partner for Dill Pickles' Save Our Planet project?"

I shake my head.

"Do you want one?"

I nod. It's an effort to talk.

"Would you like to do Pacific rainforests?" I manage to say.

Danny smiles. "Sounds good."

We eat our lunches. For me it's difficult.

Danny says, "I notice you live not too far from me."

"Yeah?"

"I see you and your kid sister go by my place all the time."

"Yeah?"

"Junk food is good for bruises." He holds out a bag of potato chips. "Help yourself."

I reach over. "Thanks."

"Take a few."

I take a few.

We're quiet for a bit while I try to chew.

Then Danny says, "I heard someone ask what the other guy looks like."

I nod. "Yeah."

He smiles. "What *does* the other guy look like, Charley?"

I shrug. "Long story." I grin, then wince. "Remind me to tell you about it some time."